MURDER
SO SWEET

J.A. WHITING

ALSO BY
J.A. WHITING

COZY MYSTERIES:

Sweet Dreams Bake Shop (Sweet Cove Cozy Mystery Book 1)

Murder So Sweet (Sweet Cove Cozy Mystery Book 2)

Sweet Secrets (Sweet Cove Cozy Mystery Book 3)

And more to come!

MYSTERIES:

The Killings (Olivia Miller Mystery - Prequel)

Red Julie (Olivia Miller Mystery - Book 1)

The Stone of Sadness (Olivia Miller Mystery - Book 2)

Justice (Olivia Miller Mystery - Book 3)
Coming Summer 2015

Summoning the Earth (Olivia Miller Mystery - Book 4)
Coming Fall 2015

For my family, with love

1

Twenty-seven year old Angie Roseland carried a platter of blueberry, carrot, and cinnamon raisin muffins to the dining room buffet table. Yogurts, fruit salad, boiled eggs, white and wheat toast, and a variety of different cereals were already displayed on the sideboard. Angie's younger sister, Ellie, had a small stack of clean plates in her hands and she placed them at one end of the table.

The girls' huge orange cat was perched high atop the China cabinet keeping watch over the morning tasks. Angie glanced up at him. "Euclid, be a good boy when the guests come down for breakfast. No hissing allowed." He flicked his tail.

The dining table was set with China plates and cups, glass goblets, linen napkins, and silver settings. A vase of fresh flowers was in the center of the table. Angie returned to the kitchen for the sugar bowl and creamer.

Ellie turned when she heard footsteps on the front staircase. "Good morning." She gave a cheerful smile to the first bed and breakfast guests to emerge from their room. "Breakfast is all ready for you."

Mr. and Mrs. Foley, a couple in their sixties, returned Ellie's greeting and headed to the dining table to take their seats. Mrs. Foley was retired from her job as a high school art teacher and Mr. Foley owned a company that installed security systems at large corporations.

"Did you sleep well?" Ellie filled their glasses with lemon water from a pitcher. The ice cubes clinked together as the water was poured.

"We slept very well," Mrs. Foley told Ellie. She placed her reading glasses on the table.

Mr. Foley took a long drink from his water glass. "The beds are very comfortable."

"I love how you've decorated the room." Mrs. Foley's eyes shined her approval. "We've stayed all over the world in different bed and breakfast inns and this one is right at the top of the list of our favorites."

Ellie's chest swelled with happiness. This was the first week that the Victorian was accepting guests and she was eager for everything to go well. She and her sisters had worked hard to prepare the rooms for maximum beauty, comfort, and relaxation. Four of the second floor bedrooms had been set aside for clients this summer so that Ellie could get her feet wet running the new enterprise.

Mrs. Foley eyed Euclid sitting high on the cabinet. "The only trouble is the cat. I'm allergic. There wasn't a mention of a cat on the bed and breakfast website."

Euclid scowled at the woman.

"Oh." Ellie's face clouded with concern. "I should have put that on there. I'll be sure to update the website with that information. I'm so sorry."

"No worries." Mrs. Foley lifted her water goblet to her lips. "I always travel with my allergy medication."

Angie winced at the mention of allergy medicine. The person who killed Professor Marion Linden, the former owner of the eighteen-room Victorian, had used allergy meds to poison her.

Angie greeted the retired couple as she set the sugar bowl and creamer on the table. She'd owned a bake shop in the small, seaside town of Sweet Cove until it closed just over three weeks ago. The building that housed Angie's café had been sold to new owners and they had other plans for the space. She was unable to find a new location for her bake shop in Sweet Cove and was resigned to having to relocate to another town, until a stroke of fortune descended. When Professor Linden passed away, she left the Victorian home and property to Angie.

The estate was now in court probate proceedings and as soon as the legal paperwork was finished, Angie would have the deed to the Victorian and the seventy-five thousand dollars also left to her by the professor. For now, Angie was acting as caretaker for the house and she'd received permission from the estate's legal representative for Ellie to run the small bed and breakfast enterprise out of the property.

"Angie." Courtney hurried into the dining room looking for her older sister. She didn't realize that two of the guests were already downstairs having their breakfast. "Oh. Good morning." She smiled at the couple and then waved to Angie to come talk to her in the foyer.

"You're up early. What's up?" Angie carried an empty tea pot.

"I'm working at the candy store today." Courtney slipped her arm around Angie to move her further away from the dining room so that they could talk privately. "Will you walk me to work? Mr. Finch is such an awful grouch he barely manages a few mutterings to me during the day. Yesterday, he made a quick comment that you were a good baker. I thought that if he saw me with you, he might be less of a sour puss to me."

Courtney had arranged a part time job working customer service at the small boutique candy store in Sweet Cove owned by Mr. Thaddeus Finch, the town grump. The candies he made were well-known and were considered some of the finest confections on the east coast. They were in demand all over the United States and Europe. Mr. Finch was as famous in Sweet Cove as his chocolates were, but his reputation was that of a miserly, bad-tempered, old coot. Most people tried to steer clear of him.

Courtney was sure she was the only person who applied for the position at Mr. Finch's store and, despite her misgivings, she accepted the job so that she would be able to contribute to the Victorian's household expenses. Courtney had graduated from college just two weeks ago and was sending out resumes for full time work, but hadn't heard anything back yet.

"I think Finch only hired me because he thinks you're a talented baker which makes no sense at all because I just work the counter, I'm not making the candy." Courtney rolled her blue eyes. "Anyway, will you walk me to work?"

Angie glanced over her shoulder at Ellie who was talking with the Foleys about sightseeing in the area. They wanted to see the museums, antique shops, and the historic district and needed recommendations for lunch and dinner at restaurants overlooking the ocean.

"Sure, I'll walk you to work. Ellie doesn't need me. I finished the morning baking. She can handle the other guests when they come down for breakfast."

Angie told Ellie that she was going into town for a little while and Ellie asked her to pick up two gallons of milk while she was there. Courtney got her lunch bag and purse, and she and Angie walked through the foyer. Courtney opened the front door and stopped short, her eyes in a wide stare. Angie looked over her sister's shoulder and stiffened.

"Hello." Attorney Jack Ford stood at the door, his hand raised, about to ring the bell. He was dressed in his usual uniform of suit jacket, pressed shirt, and bow tie. Today the tie was forest green with flecks of blue in the fabric. It was one of his more understated choices of neckware.

"What are you doing here?" Angie didn't mean for her words to sound so harsh, but she had made an agreement with the lawyer that he would always call before coming to the house. Ford had been the lawyer for the Victorian's prior owner and he was handling the estate and transfer of the house to Angie.

Angie didn't trust him. The night after Professor Linden was killed, Angie discovered that Ford was upstairs in the Victorian home searching for something in the professor's file cabinets. He snuck out of the house when Angie arrived to feed the cat. Ford claimed he had been looking for an updated will, but Angie didn't believe him. She wondered why he would sneak away if he had been in the house for any legitimate reason.

"Your sister asked me to come." Ford adjusted the cuff of his shirt.

Angie stared at Courtney, thinking she was the one who had invited Ford to the house.

"Not me." Courtney shook her head vigorously.

Ellie rushed over. "Attorney Ford. Come in."

"*You* asked him here?" Angie questioned.

Ford entered the foyer.

"I think we need to incorporate the B and B business," Ellie said. "I've read that it's a smart business move. I asked Mr. Ford to come and speak to me about the pros and cons."

Angie took Ellie's arm and moved her over near the bottom of the staircase. "Why him? Why didn't you find a different lawyer?"

Ellie answered in a hushed tone. "He's the only lawyer in Sweet Cove. I looked up lawyers who specialize in this area of law. He was rated as one of the best."

"Ellie, I don't trust him."

"Oh, I know. This is a free consultation. I just want to hear what he has to tell me. It slipped my mind to tell you. I just called him yesterday." She leaned in closer to Angie. "Don't worry. I'll keep my guard up. Maybe I can get him to spill why he was in here the night the professor died."

Attorney Ford cleared his throat.

"Don't let him out of your sight." Angie walked back to

where Courtney and Ford stood near the front door.

Ellie smiled and gestured towards the breakfast buffet. "Please come in, Mr. Ford. We're just serving breakfast. There's coffee and tea."

Ford moved into the dining room with Ellie. She looked back at her sisters and winked.

Angie let out an exasperated sigh as she and Courtney left the house and started up Beach Street to the center of town.

"I wasn't expecting to see Ford at the door." Courtney adjusted her purse's strap on her shoulder.

Feelings of distrust and anxiety rushed through Angie's body. "It was certainly a surprise for me. And, not a pleasant one."

"Why is he so weird?" The question was unanswerable.

They walked along in silence until Courtney asked, "How does someone become as ill-tempered as Mr. Finch?" Her honey blonde ponytail bounced as she walked. "He's famous at what he does. He must make tons of money. He's won awards and contests. And still, he's sour and unhappy and alone."

Angie shrugged. "Maybe he was just born that way. He's been a sour old goat since we were kids." She smiled. "Remember how he'd always scowl at us when we went in to buy candy from him when we were little?"

"Yes. It was like he hated us. I think he thought his delicious creations were being wasted on kids." Courtney chuckled. "I thought he was about a hundred years old back then."

The girls turned the corner onto Main Street and walked

by the small shops. The sun was shining and the morning air was warming up. Tourists had begun to return to the area and in another couple of weeks, the season would be in full swing with people coming to the seashore for their summer vacations.

Angie and Courtney crossed the street towards Finch Confectioners, and Courtney groaned. "Almost time to enter the grouchy old devil's den."

Angie laughed. "He can't be that bad."

"Oh, yeah? You spend eight hours with him and let me know what you think."

As they got closer to the storefront, Courtney narrowed her eyes. "The lights aren't on." She stopped walking, a look of concern on her face.

"What?" Angie sensed the tension emanating from her sister. "What's wrong? He just forgot to flick the front lights on, that's all."

Courtney shot her sister a look filled with anxiety. "He never forgets." She bolted for the door of the candy shop. She reached for the knob, yanked the door open, and rushed inside with Angie hurrying after her.

"Mr. Finch?" Courtney held her breath as she inched towards the candy making room at the rear of the store.

Angie stood in the middle of the shop, the glass-fronted candy cases circling the space. It was dead quiet. Her heart started to hammer.

Courtney took a few steps forward and halted at the threshold to the back room. Angie could see her sister's shoulders begin to shake.

"Angie, come here," Courtney whispered.   Her hand came up and covered her mouth.

Angie darted to her sister's side and followed her gaze.

Mr. Finch was on the floor on his back, lying in a pool of blood, a knife sticking out from the middle of his chest just below the ribs.

2

Courtney's breath came in gasps. She moved to Mr. Finch and knelt beside him. She reached out a trembling hand to touch his cheek. Her fingers held suspended an inch from his face. Courtney's vision started to dim and she sat back hard on her butt.

As Angie made the emergency call to the Sweet Cove police department, she crouched next to Courtney and averted her eyes from the body. She put her arms around her sister.

"Let's go back to the front. Can you stand up?" Angie put her hand on Courtney's shoulder. "Why don't we wait in the front room for the police to arrive?"

Courtney nodded. She leaned on Angie and stood. They shuffled to the customer section of the store and Angie opened the front door a crack to let in some air.

"Who would do this?" Courtney leaned against one of the candy cases and brushed her hand over her forehead.

Angie shook her head. She couldn't believe that another murder had been committed in their small town only a little more than a month after Professor Linden was killed. The professor's murderer had been caught. Now there was another killer on the loose in Sweet Cove.

A police car careened to a stop in front of the store and Chief Martin and Officer Talbot emerged and hurried to the entrance. An ambulance pulled up right behind the police car.

Courtney pointed to the back room of the shop. EMTs raced inside past the officers.

"It's Finch?" Chief Martin's face was beet red.

Angie nodded. "I walked Courtney to work this morning and...."

Courtney took over. "The lights weren't on. I knew something was wrong. Mr. Finch always puts the lights on."

"We came in and found him on the floor." Angie tilted her head in the direction of the body.

"Wait here." Chief Martin started towards the candy making room. "Or stand outside. You can sit in the cruiser if you want to. I'll need to talk to you in a minute."

The girls went outside and stood on the sidewalk. Some town residents, who owned stores next door and across the street, approached the girls. "What's happened?"

Angie said, "Mr. Finch is hurt." She just shrugged as people peppered her with questions. She didn't want to reveal the details of what had happened to Mr. Finch. Courtney said nothing.

Another police car pulled up. The officer got out and asked people not to congregate in front of the candy shop.

He stood at the door shooing the gawkers along to keep them from peeking inside. A few minutes later, Chief Martin came out and asked Angie and Courtney to come back inside so that they could talk in private.

The girls told the chief the same things they told him when he first arrived.

"How long have you been working for Mr. Finch?" The chief was writing in a small notebook.

"A week...no, ten days. I started right after graduation." Courtney had her arms wrapped around herself.

"Did you notice anyone ever arguing with Mr. Finch?" Chief Martin asked.

"No. Mr. Finch rarely came into the customer area. He stayed in the back, making the candy. He didn't interact with anyone."

"What were your duties?"

"I kept the front of the store clean, waited on customers, filled the candy cases, and shipped the candy orders out."

"Did he seem like anything was bothering him? Did Finch seem worried?" The chief's pencil was poised over the page of his notebook.

"I didn't know him well," Courtney said. "He was always the same when I was here. He didn't talk to me, just a few words about what to do. He wasn't cheerful or talkative at all. He was always sort of angry and grumpy."

"Was Mr. Finch married?" Angie asked.

The chief slipped the notebook into his back pocket. "No. He wasn't. He lived alone in his house over on Wildwood Road. We'll go over there later, to see if there's any evidence of relatives, like an address book or something.

Courtney, could you look around in here and in the back room?"

Courtney had a look of horror on her face at the chief's request. She didn't want to see Mr. Finch's dead body again.

The chief saw her pained expression. "Mr. Finch is covered over. Angie can go in with you. If you can manage it, it would be a big help."

Courtney sucked in a long breath and gave a slight nod of her head.

"Look around. See if anything looks amiss. Does anything look out of sorts? Is anything missing? Anything. No matter how subtle." The chief looked kindly at Courtney. "Can you do that?"

"Yes." Courtney inhaled a deep breath and squared her shoulders. She moved behind each of the candy cases, she checked the cash register, and looked over all of the shelves. "Nothing seems wrong here. The money is still in the drawer."

"Would you look around in back? Just don't touch anything." The chief nodded reassuringly.

"I didn't ever spend much time back there. Mr. Finch liked to work alone. But I'll go see." Courtney glanced at Angie, and her sister came up beside her. Courtney took Angie's hand and the two of them stepped into the back room.

A police officer was photographing the scene and another officer spoke into a phone. The EMTs stood off to the side talking. Courtney moved gingerly about the space being careful not to get too close to Mr. Finch's body.

The candy maker had a small built-in desk against the wall just inside the entrance to the work room. A shelf above the desk was lined with books. Courtney moved around the room, glancing at the pots and pans, the marble counter, the appliances and candy making tools. The girls opened the walk-in refrigerator, and then they looked over the items in the storage room. Nothing seemed out of place.

Courtney turned to Chief Martin. "Everything looks the same as it always does."

"Okay, thanks for checking." The chief gestured to the doorway and the girls returned to the front room.

Just as she stepped over the threshold, Courtney's face clouded. She took a backwards step into the work room and turned her head to Mr. Finch's desk. A thought played at the back of her mind, and then floated away. Courtney shrugged a shoulder.

"Anything missing or out of place?" Chief Martin asked.

"I'm not sure." Courtney took another quick look around the back room. "I knew better than to touch Mr. Finch's things. I never asked questions except what I need-ed to know to run the front of the store." An odd tingling sensation ran over Courtney's skin. She looked back at the dead body.

"Thanks, Courtney." The chief ushered the sisters to the front door of the shop. "You girls can go now, but I'll proba-bly need to talk to you again later."

"Chief." An officer called from the sidewalk.

A slender, slightly stooped, elderly man dressed in a car-digan sweater stood next to the officer. He leaned on a cane, his face pinched with worry.

The officer said, "This man says he's Thaddeus Finch's brother."

3

Chief Martin hurried to speak with the man who claimed to be Mr. Finch's brother and Courtney and Angie headed back to the Victorian.

Courtney kept her voice down. "Who would murder him? Nothing seemed to be stolen. Was it a robbery that got interrupted?"

"Who could have interrupted it?" Angie pondered. "Not us. He looked like he'd been dead for a while. Do you know what time Mr. Finch usually got to the store?"

"He was always early. I think he got there around 7am or 7:30am every day."

"And you get to work at 8:30," Angie said. "That leaves an hour or so that someone could have attacked him."

"Maybe a delivery person?" Courtney asked.

"It could have been. I wonder if maybe it wasn't a robbery at all. It could have been someone who was angry at him, had a grudge against him. He sure wasn't popular in town." Angie was trying to think of any scenario that might fit. "There might have been a business disagreement with somebody."

"Well, it must have been quite a disagreement." Thinking of Mr. Finch's stab wound, Courtney unconsciously moved her hand to her abdomen. "I can't believe he's dead. Murdered."

They turned onto the brick walkway that led to the front steps of the Victorian. "Wait until Jenna and Ellie hear this," Angie said.

"Tell Euclid," Courtney suggested, only half kidding that the cat should be consulted. "He solved Professor Linden's murder."

"Maybe the chief should deputize him. He can be the first deputy cat in history." Angie smiled, remembering how Euclid saved her from drinking poisoned tea by leaping at her and knocking the mug to the floor. "We should bring Euclid to the crime scene and see what he can discover."

The front door opened and Ellie stepped onto the porch with Attorney Ford. They shook hands and Ford came down the porch steps carrying his briefcase. He nodded at Courtney and Angie as he passed them.

Ellie gave Courtney a puzzled look. "You're home? I thought you were going to the candy shop. Why aren't you at work?"

Courtney walked up onto the porch. "We need to tell you something. It isn't good."

Ellie's eyes widened. "Oh, no." After last month's murder of Professor Linden, she'd been hoping to settle into a comfortable rhythm running the bed and breakfast with no troubles and no worries to interfere.

Angie came up the steps behind Courtney. "Where's Jenna? We can tell you both at the same time."

Ellie held her hands together and squeezed them. She was the family worrier. Her sisters teased her that if worrying ever became an Olympic sport then she would win the gold medal. "Jenna's working in her shop."

They headed along the wraparound porch to the rear of the Victorian where Jenna used one of the rooms to design and construct her jewelry. She ran an internet business selling her pieces and also had two cases of her designs at the front of the shop for walk-in sales. Jenna was hunched over her table near the windows using a tool to close a clasp on a necklace. Euclid, their giant orange cat, was curled up asleep on a corner of the desk. Jenna and the cat glanced up when they heard the girls come in.

"Hey. What's up?" Jenna's light brown hair was in a braid hanging over her shoulder. Euclid stood up and stretched. Jenna smiled at her sisters, but it quickly faded when she saw the looks on their faces. "What's happened now?"

"Exactly." Ellie sat in a chair next to Jenna waiting for the bad news.

Courtney rubbed at her forehead and temples. "Mr. Finch is dead. We found him. Murdered."

"What?" Jenna nearly leaped from her chair.

Ellie's hand cradled the side of her face. "Not another murder. How can this be?"

Angie sat on the small sofa that Jenna had placed near the entrance to her shop. "I walked Courtney to work this morning. When we got there, the place was quiet. The front door was unlocked. We went in."

Courtney sat down next to Angie. "I looked in the back room. He was on the floor, bleeding."

"He'd been stabbed," Angie said.

Jenna and Ellie both gasped.

"What on earth?" Ellie clutched the arms of her chair.

"Are there suspects?" Jenna put her jewelry tool down next to the necklace she was putting together.

Angie and Courtney shrugged. Euclid walked over and jumped onto Courtney's lap.

"Finch was a foul tempered creature." Jenna was thinking out loud. "Maybe he rubbed someone the wrong way?"

Ellie gave Jenna an exasperated look. "Well, he *must* have rubbed someone the wrong way. He's been murdered."

Jenna got up and started pacing. "It could have been a robber. Some nut. It doesn't have to be someone with a grudge against him." She turned to her sisters. "The killer doesn't have to be someone living in Sweet Cove this time. Maybe the killer is long gone." She hoped, anyway.

Ellie sighed. "Two killings in just over a month. I hope this isn't going to scare tourists off from coming here this summer. It could kill the town's economy."

Courtney scratched Euclid's cheeks. "*Kill* the economy? Poor choice of words, Sis." She leaned against the sofa back. "Maybe it will actually draw people to town. Lots of people love murder mysteries."

Ellie rolled her eyes.

"Was anything missing from the candy store?" Jenna asked. "Was money stolen?"

"It didn't seem like it," Angie said.

Courtney ran her hand over Euclid's luxurious fur. "Everything seemed to be in place. The money in the cash register looked untouched. I didn't notice anything missing in the shop."

Euclid's hazel green eyes made contact with Courtney.

"I wonder if someone stole something I didn't notice." Courtney had a faraway look on her face.

"Maybe it was someone with a grudge against Finch?" Angie wondered.

"A grudge?" Ellie had a look of disbelief. "Would someone murder a person over some stupid grudge?"

"I guess people have killed for less." Angie gave Courtney's shoulder a squeeze and stood up. "Chief Martin said he'd probably want to talk with us again later. Maybe he'll have some ideas about what happened." She looked over at Ellie. "How did it go with Attorney Ford?"

"It went well. He gave me some good information. I have a folder with things I want to go over with all of you. See if you think it's a good idea to incorporate the business. And I never let Ford out of my sight. He had another appointment so I didn't get to pursue why he was in the house the night Professor Linden died." Ellie stood and moved to the doorway that led to the hall. "I need to get back to the dining room to see to the guests." She glanced at Courtney. "I guess you need a new job now. Want to help me with the B and B duties?"

Courtney followed Ellie into the hall. "Yes, anything to get my mind off of seeing Mr. Finch with a knife sticking out of his gut."

Angie winced at the image. She moved over to stand near Jenna's work table, her face serious. She kept her voice low. "You know, I wonder if Courtney is developing powers."

Jenna's eyebrows went up. "What do you mean?"

"When we got close to the shop this morning, I could almost feel something coming off of her, some kind of energy. She seemed, I don't know, like hyper aware. She seemed to sense that something was wrong."

"Could it just have been her intuition?"

"It's possible." Angie looked out the window, thinking. "But it seemed more than that. I think I felt something similar when Lisa tried to poison me."

Jenna sat in her chair and fiddled with a tool on her desk. "Courtney told us that Nana said we would probably develop powers as we get older. Maybe Courtney's powers are bubbling up." Jenna turned and eyed Euclid still curled comfortably on the sofa. "Do you ever get the feeling that cat knows stuff?"

Euclid raised his head like he was interested in what Angie's answer would be.

"All the time," Angie replied.

The sisters stared at the big orange cat as he placed his head on his paws and closed his eyes.

Just then, Courtney hurried back into Jenna's shop from the hallway. "You won't believe who's checking into the B and B."

4

Jenna and Angie asked in unison. "Who is it?"

"Mr. Finch's brother."

"He's here?" Angie moved to the doorway where Courtney stood.

"Yeah." Courtney turned and started out of the room. "You better come into the dining room because Ellie looks like she's about to faint."

Jenna chuckled as Angie followed Courtney down the hallway and into the foyer. Ellie and Mr. Finch were sitting side by side at the dining table. He was filling in his information on the check-in card. He lifted his head and adjusted his glasses when he heard the girls come in.

His mouth opened in surprise. "You? Weren't you both at the candy shop?"

"You're Mr. Finch's brother?" Angie moved to shake his hand. "I'm Angie Roseland, Ellie's sister."

"I'm Victor Finch."

Ellie was pale. "This is our sister, Courtney."

Courtney nodded. "I worked for your brother. Part time. I just started about a week ago." She shook hands with the man. "I'm sorry for your loss."

"Thank you." The man mumbled. "I'm in shock." Worry lines creased his forehead.

"Can I get you some tea?" Courtney offered.

"Oh, yes, please. I would appreciate that." The old man placed his glasses on the table.

Angie sat down across from Finch and Courtney headed for the kitchen to get the tea.

"Are you from nearby?" Angie asked.

The man gave a vigorous shake of his head. "My, no. I live in California. I've never been to the east coast. Thaddeus and I grew up in Chicago."

"When I took Mr. Finch's reservation, I didn't connect him to the candy store Mr. Finch." Ellie's shaky fingers reached for Finch's credit card where he had placed it on the table. "I'll just go run this through. I'll be right back." She went into the small den off of the hallway that she was using as her office.

"Were you the one who found my brother?" Mr. Finch's hands shook and he placed them in his lap.

Angie nodded. "I was walking Courtney to work. We both found your brother. I called the police."

Mr. Finch let out a long sigh. "It's ironic, really." He made eye contact with Angie. "Thaddeus and I...we've been estranged. For a very long time." He looked down at his hands. "I came to try to patch things up between us." He gave Angie a small wistful smile. "I guess I waited just a day too long."

"I'm sorry. It must be very hard for you. Did you just arrive in town today?"

"Yes. This morning." Mr. Finch glanced about the room. "You have a lovely home here."

"Thank you," Angie said. "We've only recently moved in."

Courtney returned with a tray. She placed the teapot, cups, small plates, spoons, a creamer and sugar bowl on the table. "Here are some apple squares Angie made this morning." She put the plate of treats in the center of the table and moved to the hutch where she removed some linen napkins and put one in front of everyone's place. Courtney poured tea into each person's cup.

When Ellie came back and sat down, Angie asked Mr. Finch, "How did your brother end up in Sweet Cove?"

Mr. Finch had a blank expression on his face. He blinked a few times. "I have no idea. I only recently found out he lived here."

"You hadn't kept in touch?" Ellie lifted her tea cup to her lips.

"No. Sadly." Finch took a bite of his apple square and nodded to Angie. "You're a very good baker."

Angie thanked him. They made idle chit chat while they drank their tea.

Finch lifted his napkin to his lips. "If you'll excuse me, I'd like to go up and lie down for a little while."

Ellie stood up. "I have your key. I'll show you to your room." She walked to the foyer and picked up Finch's small suitcase, gestured for him to follow her, and they started up the staircase.

Once they were out of earshot, Courtney leaned forward. "Do you think he killed his brother?"

Angie's eyes widened. "How could he? He's old. He doesn't seem very strong."

"Does it take a lot of strength to stab someone? What if he took Mr. Finch by surprise?"

"I don't know." Angie had never considered such a thing, but maybe with a sharp knife, strength wouldn't be a requirement.

Courtney glanced over her shoulder to be sure Finch wasn't coming back downstairs. "It's a coincidence isn't it? The brothers haven't seen each other for forever." She pointed upstairs. "Then this Mr. Finch shows up, and the other Mr. Finch, dead Finch, gets killed."

"It is suspicious." Angie thought for a moment. "But it would be stupid to do such a thing. Show up out of the blue and your brother suddenly dies? And if he did kill him, why would he hang around here? Why not just take off?"

Courtney leaned back in her chair. "Maybe he came for something, but can't find it, so he's hanging around." Her deep blue eyes grew wide. "What if he's after something? Who knows what? Dead Finch's house? The candy store? His bank account? Dead Finch must have lots of money since he's been so successful."

The doorbell rang and Courtney rose to answer it.

Their friend Tom stepped inside. "Hey, Courtney. Angie."

Angie went over to greet Tom. He owned a construction

and renovation business. He was going to do the renovations on the Victorian to house Angie's bake shop once she received the money from the inheritance.

"I was passing by. I want to take some more measurements for that door you want installed upstairs."

"Oh, yeah?" Angie eyed him with suspicion. "Jenna's in her shop." Tom and Jenna had been flirting with each other for over a month.

Tom's cheeks flushed a tiny bit pink. "I didn't just come by to see Jenna."

"Right." Courtney called from the dining room where she was clearing the dishes from the table. She gave Tom a sly wink.

Angie took Tom's arm and herded him down the hallway towards Jenna's work room. "You heard about Mr. Finch?"

"What do you mean?"

Angie told Tom that Finch had been murdered and that his brother had just checked in to the B and B.

"Another murder in town?" Tom stood still, flabbergasted. "What's going on?"

"I know, huh?" Angie ran her hand over her hair. "They'll be changing the town's name to Murder So Sweet Cove."

A look of horror passed over Tom's face. "Dear God."

They started walking down the hallway. "You want a coffee?" Angie asked.

"That'd be great. I sure miss going to your shop every morning." Tom had been a regular at Angie's Sweet Dreams Bake Shop before she had to close it.

"Would you like a piece of pecan pie to go with the coffee?" Angie headed into the kitchen.

"You bet I would." Tom smiled and rubbed his tummy. "I'm glad I stopped by."

Angie grinned. "I'll bring it to you. Go see Jenna."

"You don't have to tell me twice." Tom winked. He headed to the end of the hall and into Jenna's shop.

5

The next morning, Angie and Courtney loaded the trunk of Angie's car with cakes and pies. While she was waiting for the inheritance money to come through so that the renovations on the Victorian could begin to outfit her café, Angie had contracted with several restaurants in town to provide them with desserts, muffins, and breakfast breads. She couldn't wait until her bake shop could open in part of the Victorian, but in the mean time, she could keep herself busy baking for town establishments.

"You sure you don't need help with the deliveries?" Courtney slammed the trunk. "I'm sure Ellie can manage without me for an hour or two."

"Thanks, but I can do it." Angie reached in her pocket for the car key. "I know there's a lot to do for the B and B today." She opened the car door. "It's going to be a warm day. Want to go to the beach this afternoon for a little while? Maybe Jenna and Ellie can get away for a couple of hours."

"I'd love that. I'll see you when you get back."

Angie sat down in the driver's seat and backed the car into the street. She waved at Courtney as she drove away to her first stop.

Angie parked in front of The Pirate's Den restaurant, checked her list, and removed two cakes and two pie boxes from the trunk. Bessie Lindquist, the owner, saw her coming and hurried to open the door of the restaurant for Angie. She took the two top boxes from Angie to lighten the load. Two waitresses came over and carried the desserts to the kitchen.

"Your treats are big favorites here." Bessie pulled a silver pen from her apron pocket and handed it to Angie. "You want some tea or coffee?"

"No thanks. I have a bunch of deliveries to make." Angie made a note on the receipt and handed it to Bessie to sign.

Bessie and her husband had owned the Pirate's Den for over twenty years. She was petite and had small, pretty features. Her silvery blonde, short hair framed her face. Bessie glanced through the big front windows to the Finch Confectioners storefront across the street. "You found Finch? You found the body?"

"Courtney and I did, yes."

Bessie shook her head. "Can't say I'm sorry he's gone."

Angie's eyes widened and Bessie added, "Oh you know what I mean. I feel bad he was killed of course, but he was a nasty old thing. Don't think I ever heard a pleasant word from that man."

"Do you know anything about him?"

Bessie made a face. "Really? I don't think I do. I've had the restaurant here across from his store for more than twenty years and I can't think of anything I know about the man. Isn't that sad?"

"Maybe he didn't want to be known," Angie offered.

"That's even sadder, then." Bessie shook her head.

Lindsay, the assistant manager and waitress, was working at a table near the window putting the daily specials sheet into the menus. She was in her thirties and had shoulder-length auburn hair. Two years ago, Lindsay was about eighty pounds overweight when she decided she wanted to change her ways and live a healthier lifestyle. She took up running and biking with a vengeance. Now fit and strong, Lindsay was a competitive tri-athlete. "I agree with you, Bessie. Finch was a monster. I worked at the candy shop for a month about two years ago. It was the longest month of my life."

"What did he do?" Angie had heard Courtney's complaints about Finch and wondered what Lindsay's experience was.

"I was heavy back then. He made nasty comments about my weight. He said the customers would worry that there wouldn't be anything left for them because I must be eating all the candy. He didn't want to hire me because I was heavy, but no one else applied for the job." Her face clouded over thinking about working for Finch. "I wish I hadn't applied. He accused me of stealing from him, money, supplies, candy. He often docked my pay. When I complained, he would point to the door. He even reported me to the police department, told them I was stealing from him. I needed the job so I put up with it until I found something else. I left there in a hurry as soon as I got another job." Lindsay's eyes flashed with anger. "He couldn't keep workers. No one could stand him. He was really paranoid, too. Sometimes he kept the door to the back work room locked. He was always wary about people, like he thought someone *was* out to get him." She stopped what she was doing, holding one of the menu inserts in mid-air. "Well, I guess someone was out to get him." Lindsay returned to her task and continued, "I was out running the other day. I stopped in front of the candy shop to catch my breath after my run. The door to Finch's store was open. I could hear a heated discussion in there."

Angie perked up. "Could you hear what they were saying?"

Lindsay said, "Not really. It was the loud voices and the tone that caught my attention. I wasn't really able to understand what they were saying to each other."

"When was this?" Angie moved closer to the table where Lindsay was working.

"The day before he was killed." Lindsay kept at her task without looking up.

"Did you see who Finch was arguing with?"

"No. It was a man though, I could tell that."

Angie wanted more information. "What age would you say the man was? Did he sound old? Young?"

Lindsay yawned. "Hmm…maybe he was older…definitely not a young guy."

"Did you notice any cars parked in front of the candy shop that day?" Angie hoped this would lead to something.

"Maybe? I think there was a car."

"Can you remember anything about it? The color? The make?"

Lindsay shook her head. "I couldn't say for sure. I wasn't paying attention."

Angie wanted to sigh, but held it in. "What about what they were arguing about? Are you sure you couldn't hear any part of what they said? Anything at all? Did some words stand out?"

Lindsay's face scrunched up as she thought about it. "I don't know…maybe someone said something about a picture? But that can't be right." Lindsay shrugged.

"What time was it when you were near the candy store?" Angie thought this would be a question that Lindsay could answer.

Lindsay looked up. "I finished my run around 7:30."

"Did you tell the police what you heard?"

"The police came in to talk to us about the murder. I told them what I heard."

Angie nodded. "Good. Maybe it will help. Well, if you think of anything else, will you let me know? I'll be back on Wednesday to drop off some more desserts." Angie said goodbye and left to go to her car. She didn't want to be late for her other deliveries.

Just as she was getting in, a man's voice called her name. She turned to see Josh Williams walking briskly across the street to her.

Josh had a broad smile on his face. Angie felt her muscles melting at the sight of him.

"Hey. How are you?"

His blue eyes warmed Angie. "I'm good. Doing deliveries."

"I'm back from Maine for a while." Josh leaned against

Angie's car. "I managed to extract myself from my brother's tentacles."

Angie smiled. "How's the project going?"

"Slow. Davis drives a hard bargain. I think the deal is fine, but he always wants better terms so negotiations drag on." Josh shrugged. "I came back to check on the resort. The new manager seems to be having problems." Josh and his brother Davis were property developers and they owned a high-end resort located on Robin's Point at the southern end of Sweet Cove. They had recently replaced the resort's previous manager with someone new.

"Is the new manager having a hard time settling into the job?"

"I'm not sure what the problem is, really. There have been some complaints." Josh brushed aside his concerns about the manager. "I'll be around town for a week or so, maybe two weeks. If you have some time, would you like to try that bike ride again someday?"

"I would." Angie smiled. "Hopefully this time there won't be a typhoon or other natural disaster." Josh had invited Angie to go for a bike ride on the day after she closed her bake shop, but the day dawned with a deluge of rain and wind which didn't let up until nightfall. They had to cancel the ride and the next day Josh had to go to Maine with his brother to pursue a land development deal.

Josh gave a hearty laugh. "I certainly hope not. We deserve a sunny day after last time."

They exchanged numbers and Josh told Angie he would be in touch as soon as he had a chance to see what needed to be done about the resort. They parted ways, and Angie got into her car to make her next delivery. She wondered if Josh had heard about Mr. Finch.

Yellow police tape was tied across the door to Finch Confectioner's and as Angie attached her seat belt, she thought she noticed a light on in the back room of the store. She was just about to insert her key into the ignition, when Chief Martin emerged from the candy store. He waved to Angie with his index finger in the air to indicate that he wanted her to wait. Angie rolled her window down as the chief crossed the street and greeted her.

"I understand Mr. Finch is staying at the B and B." The chief leaned down so he could speak to Angie in the car.

"He is. He checked in yesterday." Angie's hands rested on the steering wheel.

"Did you talk to him?" the chief asked.

"Not much. We had tea with him, but he said he was tired and went up to his room to rest. I don't know if he went out for dinner or not. I didn't see him this morning." Angie moved her hands to her lap. "Poor man. He just missed reuniting with his brother."

The chief said, "He mentioned that to me when I spoke with him the day of the murder."

"Mr. Finch told us that he and his brother were estranged. He hadn't seen him for years."

The chief reached up and adjusted his cap. "Did he say if there are other relatives?"

"We didn't ask him about that."

"I need to talk to him." The chief glanced at his watch then looked at Angie. "It's too early to barge in on him now. Are you going somewhere?"

Angie looked surprised at the question. "I'm making my deliveries."

A blank expression was on the chief's face.

"I've contracted to do bakery items and desserts for some of the restaurants and hotels in town," Angie clarified.

"Oh." The chief understood. "Excellent. That's a good idea until you open your bake shop in the Victorian." The chief let out a sigh. "I'll be glad when you're open again. I miss the shop."

"It won't be until September I'm afraid." Angie got the feeling the chief wanted to say something more. She thought he seemed distracted. She waited for a few moments, but the chief didn't say anything else. "I should get going. I have more deliveries to make."

"When will you finish the deliveries? What time will you be home?"

"In about an hour. Maybe a little longer." Angie adjusted herself in the driver's seat so she could better face the chief. "Do you need something?"

The chief scratched his chin. "I'd like it if you were around when I talk to Mr. Finch."

"Me?"

The chief nodded. "And Courtney, too. I need to go over to Finch's house and look around. The dead Mr. Finch's house." He shifted his feet.

Angie thought the chief was acting a bit odd. "Is something wrong?"

"Huh? No. Could you come along to the inspection of Finch's house?"

"Me?" Angie's eyebrows raised in surprise. "Why?"

"I'd like Courtney to come too. Extra pairs of eyes, that's all."

Angie narrowed her blue eyes at the chief. "Wouldn't other police officers be more helpful?" She was puzzled by why Chief Martin would want her and Courtney to be around when he inspected Mr. Finch's property.

"Maybe." Chief Martin shrugged a shoulder. "Maybe not."

Angie eyed him. "Is there something you're not telling me?"

The chief checked his watch again. "Can we talk later? Can I meet you at the Victorian in about two hours? That'll give you time to do your deliveries." He started to walk away. "I'll see you then."

As Angie watched him cross the street, she realized her mouth was hanging open and she shut it. She couldn't imagine what was going on. Why had the chief asked her and Courtney to be present when he spoke with Finch? And why did he ask them to join him when he visited the home of the late Mr. Finch. Shaking her head, Angie started the car and headed to her next stop.

6

Angie pulled into the Victorian's driveway and saw Courtney and Euclid on the front porch. Euclid sat supervising Courtney as she was taking freshly washed linens from one laundry basket, folding them, and placing them in another basket.

Angie parked and walked over to the porch.

Courtney waved. "Hey, Sis. What's cookin'?" Courtney reached for another sheet. "It's like a summer day. Are you still planning on going to the beach later?"

Angie gave Euclid a pat on the head and he leaned into her hand for more scratching. "I'd like to." She sat in one of the porch rockers.

"But?" Courtney placed the last folded sheet into the basket and sat down in the rocker next to Angie.

Euclid jumped onto Angie's lap. "After I made my morning delivery to the Pirate's Den, I was sitting in my car and

Chief Martin saw me and came over to talk." She told Courtney that the chief wanted both of them to be present when he came to speak to Mr. Finch and when he went to make a visit to the late Mr. Finch's house.

"Us? Why?" Courtney's eyebrows furrowed in confusion. "How could we be of any use?"

"I have no idea." Angie sighed. She didn't want to be involved in another murder case.

"Well, I think it's kind of cool." Courtney sat up in her chair and chuckled. "Will we get a police badge?" She turned to Euclid. "What do you think of that, Euclid? We're being brought in to help solve the case."

Euclid purred.

Angie patted the big orange cat's back. "I don't think we're being brought in as detectives."

"Well," Courtney said, "consultants then." She looked at Angie. "But, why?"

"Do you think it's because you worked for Finch?"

"I only worked there for ten days. What could I know?" Courtney looked out over the front lawn. "I guess we'll find out soon why Chief Martin wants us around ... because here he comes."

The chief pulled his police vehicle to a stop in front of the Victorian and strode across the grass to the porch where he greeted the girls. He climbed the steps.

Angie was still patting Euclid. "I just got home a few minutes ago. I haven't been inside yet. I don't know where Mr. Finch is, but Ellie will know. Shall we go in?"

"Ah, in a minute. I'd like a chance to talk to you both."

Angie couldn't remember ever seeing Chief Martin

looking so uncomfortable. He shifted his feet and didn't make eye contact with either one of them. He leaned against the porch railing. Euclid lifted his head to stare at the chief.

"What's wrong?" Courtney asked. The chief's behavior made her nervous. "You aren't suspecting me of killing Mr. Finch are you?"

The chief's eyes went wide. "No. That's not it." He shook his head vigorously and took a deep breath. "I…." He shoved his hands in his pockets. "I … knew your grandmother."

Angie wondered what on earth this was going to be about. When Chief Martin mentioned Nana, a chill skittered over her skin.

Euclid sat up.

The chief said, "We were friends." A tiny stick lay on the porch floor and he poked at it with the toe of his boot. "She was, um, helpful to me."

"You mean with her powers?" Courtney blurted. Angie shot her sister a look of horror for mentioning such a private, and what many would consider crazy, matter.

Relief washed over the chief's face.

"Did she help you with cases?" Courtney sat up eager to hear what the chief had to say.

"Sometimes." Chief Martin glanced at Angie. "Am I saying anything that you don't know?"

Angie let out a tiny breath. "I just recently learned that my grandmother had some sort of … gift. Courtney knew a little about it when she was just a kid. But we don't know much."

The chief visibly relaxed. "Do you…?" The chief didn't finish his sentence.

"You mean do we have it?" Courtney asked. "The gift?"
The chief nodded.

Courtney pulled her legs up under her. "Angie's powers are getting stronger, but they're still new and she doesn't know anything about what she might be able to do. Jenna and Ellie don't show anything. I don't have anything either. Yet."

Angie looked over at her sister with a serious expression. "You felt something was wrong when we approached the candy store."

Courtney thought back on the morning. "Yeah, I did. Maybe I sensed it?" She smiled at the chief. "Is this why you want us to be around when you talk to Mr. Finch?"

"I thought it might be helpful." He seemed sheepish about it.

"What did Nana do?" Angie asked as Euclid stretched on her lap. "How did she help you?"

"She helped with cases that were going nowhere. She'd talk things over with me. Sometimes she'd go with me to a crime scene or stand behind the one-way window when we questioned a suspect." The chief adjusted his cap. "She was respected. She worked with detectives from a number of towns. In Boston, too."

"Boston?" Angie couldn't believe that detectives would believe in this stuff. "Did she really help?"

The chief nodded. "Your grandmother once told me that she sensed all of you girls would develop some, ah, skills. She was sure of it."

"Really?" Courtney was excited. "That's great."

Angie said, "I'm not sure Ellie would agree with you

about that." She made eye contact with the chief. "Who else knows this about Nana?"

"Only some law enforcement agents. They keep it to themselves. It isn't widely known. I know the most."

"Can we keep it that way?" Angie didn't care to have unwanted attention from people knowing what her grandmother could do. She still didn't understand any of it herself.

"Absolutely." Chief Martin nodded.

Angie cleared her throat. "And if we can help you in some strange way, will you keep that to yourself?"

The chief said, "You have my word."

"Okay." Angie turned to Courtney. "I think we better not broadcast this stuff to people. We don't even know what we're dealing with yet. Later today, we should tell Jenna and Ellie what Chief Martin just told us about Nana."

Courtney nodded. "Can we go talk to Mr. Finch now?"

The three of them headed inside. As Courtney was about to open the door, the chief spoke, his voice a little shaky. He glanced at Euclid. "Could that cat come in with us?"

Angie gave the chief a look of surprise mixed with equal parts wonder and alarm. "Why?"

Chief Martin gave a pathetic shrug.

Euclid stood up, jumped down from the chair, walked proudly to the open door, and entered the foyer in front of the humans, his huge orange tail flicking from side to side.

* * *

Inside the house, the unusual quartet entered the dining room where Mr. Finch, dressed in a shirt and tie and suit jacket, sat at the table, drinking tea and reading a newspaper. He glanced up, his eyes moving over the group. "Hello."

"Can we join you, Mr. Finch?" Angie stepped forward.

"Please." Finch gestured to the seats around the table.

They all sat down around the dining table. Euclid jumped up to the top of the China cabinet.

"How are you doing, Mr. Finch?" Courtney sat across from him. "Did you sleep okay?"

"I don't travel often and I can be restless in a new place, but the bed and the room are so comfortable I slept extremely well." He lifted his tea cup to his lips. "Is there any news about my brother, Chief Martin?"

"We're continuing our investigation."

Ellie came into the room. "Oh, you're all here. I'll bring some more cups." She turned to go back to the kitchen.

"Would you mind if I asked you some questions, Mr. Finch?" Chief Martin asked.

"I don't mind at all. I want to do what I can to help." Finch lifted his napkin to his mouth and wiped his lips.

"When was the last time you saw your brother?"

Finch leaned back and looked off into space. "I don't recall." He was quiet for several moments, thinking. "When we were in our early twenties. That's the last time I saw him."

"That was some time ago," Chief Martin said.

"Time flies and leaves us in its wake." Finch placed his hand around his tea cup.

"Had you spoken with your brother? Did you keep in contact?"

"No. To my great sorrow."

Courtney didn't think Finch's words fit the lack of emotion that he showed. She thought he seemed very business-like while claiming heartache over the loss of his brother. It didn't ring true to her.

"Are you retired? What did you do for a living?" The chief was writing in a small notebook he had placed on the table.

"I spent my working life as a teacher. A mathematics teacher."

Euclid stood up on the China cabinet and let out a long, low hiss. Everyone turned to look at the cat. Ellie had just entered the room carrying a tray of mugs. "Euclid, stop that hissing." She placed a mug at everyone's place.

"What's wrong with the cat?" Mr. Finch asked.

Angie said, "His previous owner was a mathematics professor." After the words were out of her mouth, she felt foolish for saying such a silly thing.

"He speaks English?" Finch inquired.

Angie wasn't sure how to answer that question.

Courtney said, "He understands what we say. Euclid is very intelligent."

The chief tried to get the questioning back on track. "Do you have any other relatives?"

"I'm afraid not." Finch shook his head sadly.

"Are you married, Mr. Finch?"

"I never found the proper match."

Angie was amazed how little information was actually coming out of this conversation. She had learned very little about Finch despite the Chief's questions.

"May I ask what the reason was for your estrangement from your brother?" The chief leaned into the table slightly, his pen poised in the air.

Finch gave a small chuckle. "It was so long ago. You may find this odd, but I don't recall."

The girls flashed a quick look at Chief Martin. Courtney wondered how Finch could forget what caused a rift so great that he and his brother hadn't spoken for fifty years. Angie thought that it must be something very troubling or important if Finch pretended that he had forgotten the reason that he and his brother had a falling out.

"Did your brother know you were coming to see him?" Angie asked.

Finch looked over the rims of his glasses at Angie. "I thought it best to surprise him."

The chief straightened up in his seat. "We're going to visit your brother's home later today. You may accompany us, if you'd like."

"Yes, I would like to join you." Finch pushed his seat back from the table. "I'd like to go to my room now and rest. Would you excuse me?"

The chief gave a slight nod. "We'll be leaving for your brother's house in about two hours."

"I'll be ready." Finch stood, walked slowly to the staircase, and clutching the banister and leaning on his cane, slowly pulled himself up the flight of stairs.

"That was a bunch of nothing," Courtney whispered.

"Exactly." The chief looked at each girl. "Did you get anything from the encounter?"

Angie shook her head. "I didn't sense anything, no more than what anyone else would feel from evasive answers."

"I didn't get anything from him either." As Courtney

turned to look up at the cabinet, she asked, "How about you, Euclid?"

Euclid was not in his usual place on top of the cabinet. Courtney, Angie, and the chief craned their necks to look into the foyer. Euclid sat on a side table, eagerly looking out the window, flicking his tail.

"Guess he lost interest in the proceedings." Chief Martin stood and told the girls, "Maybe at Finch's house you'll sense something." He gestured to the second floor. "This Mr. Finch didn't have much to share, did he?"

"It makes me suspicious." Courtney stood up and folded her arms over her chest.

"Courtney has been suspicious of him since he arrived here," Angie told the chief.

"Maybe there's reason for that. I'll be back in a couple of hours. We'll head over to take a look around the house."

The chief thanked the girls for trying, and they walked him to the door. When Courtney opened it, a medium-sized black cat with a white spot on her chest sat on the porch in front of them.

"Who's this?" Angie bent and held out her hand. The cat moved closer, sniffed Angie's fingers and rubbed her cheeks on them. "What a friendly girl."

Euclid appeared beside Angie. He and the black cat sniffed noses. Euclid turned and the cat followed him into the house.

"Hey." Courtney went to pick up the new cat. Euclid arched his back and hissed at her. "Bad boy. No hissing at me." Courtney looked at Angie. "What should we do?'

Angie waved her hand at the two cats. "Let her stay.

She'll probably ask to go home soon enough."

The cats disappeared into the house.

"Looks like she's come to stay." The chief walked down the porch steps to go to his car. "I'll pick you up in two hours."

7

The chief's police car pulled into the driveway and Angie, Courtney, and Mr. Finch came down off the porch. Angie held Mr. Finch's arm. He had his cane in one hand. The chief opened the vehicle's back door and helped Finch onto the back seat. Courtney took the front passenger side. "This is only the second time I've been in a police car." She looked all around.

"That's good news." Chief Martin gave Courtney a smile. "I'm glad to hear that you haven't been in a police car other than with me driving." He started the car, backed out, and drove several miles to the late Thaddeus Finch's house.

Victor Finch craned his neck as the car approached his brother's home. The house was a small, neatly tended ranch with an attached two-car garage. There were no flowers around the property, but the lawn and bushes were trimmed and healthy. Chief Martin pulled into the driveway and parked in front of one of the garage bays.

The chief, holding a camera, opened the car doors for Angie, Finch, and Courtney. The four of them approached the house.

"It's what I expected of Thaddeus." Finch glanced around. "Nothing ostentatious. Simple and functional. He wasn't one for extravagance."

The chief opened the front door and he and Courtney went inside. Angie helped Finch up the few front stairs. When they entered the house, Angie's eyes widened.

There was a small foyer with beautiful Italian ceramic tiles on the floor. The space to the right ran from the front to the back of the house and had a gleaming hardwood floor and cathedral ceilings. The walls were cream and the room was furnished sparsely with a Scandinavian style sofa, two chairs, and a glass coffee table positioned before a tiled fireplace. The rear wall of the room was all glass affording a full view of the backyard lawn and trees. Contemporary artwork of vivid colors hung on the walls. The effect was stunning and it echoed being in a high-end art gallery.

"I wasn't expecting this." Courtney stood in the middle of the room gazing about.

Mr. Finch limped around the room leaning on his cane, his eyes wide. Chief Martin took photographs of the space. Angie walked over to look at the paintings. The place looked like a layout in a high-end architectural magazine. Angie noticed that personal belongings were lacking in the room, no photographs, no books, no knick-knacks of any kind. Except for the paintings, the room was sterile and cold.

The four of them entered an enormous all white kitchen. Everything was neatly in place. Inside the cabinets, white dishes stood at the ready, glasses of different sizes lined up like soldiers. Everything was clean. No crumbs, no clutter. Nothing even looked used.

"Well," Angie said, "it sure doesn't look like our kitchen."

"It's kind of creepy," Courtney whispered. "Where's all the…stuff?"

The chief opened a cabinet and pulled out the trash can which glided smoothly on metal runners. There were just two crumpled paper towels at the bottom.

"Did Finch really live here?" Angie moved her palm over the granite counters. "It's like no one ever used the place."

Courtney opened the fridge. "There's food in the fridge at least."

They continued into the other rooms, each one clean and neat and Spartan. Dead Finch's clothes hung in the closet, lined up by color, which only included shades of black and gray. Moving from room to room, the chief opened drawers and closets. There weren't any spaces stuffed with papers or clutter. No bills, no letters, no newspapers. There were no cars in the pristine garage space.

Courtney asked Mr. Finch, "Was your brother always a neat freak?"

Finch took a deep breath. "He always wanted things neat, to have control. It was important to him."

After looking through the other rooms, they returned to the living room.

"Do you like the paintings?" Finch asked no one in particular.

"I like the colors," Angie said. "But I'm not really a big fan of abstract art."

"I think they're striking." Courtney gazed at the shapes and colors.

"Then you have good taste, Miss Courtney." Finch kept his eyes on the wall's displays. "These pieces of art are very valuable."

The chief moved closer to Mr. Finch. "Are they?"

Finch nodded. "We'd better remember to arm the house alarm when we leave."

"You're familiar with abstract art?" Angie asked.

"I am." He gestured to the paintings. "My brother has amassed quite a collection."

Angie thought she noticed the shimmer of a tear in Mr. Finch's eye, and she instinctively put her hand on his arm. The skitter of something flew over her skin and for a half second an image tried to form in her mind, but in a flash, it was gone.

"The paintings are valuable?" Chief Martin asked as he photographed more of the room.

"Very." Finch's voice was soft.

The chief was about to shift his camera towards the far wall when he asked, "How valuable? Are you able to estimate?"

Finch cleared his throat. "One or two million dollars worth. At least."

Angie's mouth dropped open.

The chief whirled back to Finch and gaped at him.

Courtney's eyes went wide. "Who knew selling candy was so lucrative?"

8

The four sisters relaxed in the large family room at the back of the house that they had made into their private space. Courtney and Angie told Jenna and Ellie about the visit to the late Mr. Finch's house and the art collection that was inside.

"That's amazing." Jenna passed a bowl of popcorn to Angie. "How did he afford it all?"

"Maybe he bought the paintings when the artists were unknowns," Ellie suggested. "Then their value increased over the years."

"That's possible." Angie shifted and rested her head back against the sofa. "When we were at the house, I thought I felt something from Mr. Finch ... sadness...a loss. I only sensed it for a moment and then the feeling was gone. I wonder what it was."

"Could it be a memory he had? And you picked up on

it?" Courtney lounged sideways on one of the chairs, her legs hanging over one of the arms.

Angie's comment about sensing something from Finch led to her and Courtney telling their sisters what Chief Martin had said about Nana helping the police with cases and that Nana was sure all four of them would develop powers of some sort. The discussion centered on when it might happen to each of them and what kind of skills they might have.

Ellie was not on board. The idea gave her the creeps.

Courtney told Ellie, "Maybe you inherited Mom's aversion to powers. She didn't want anything to do with it either."

Jenna considered. "Of the four of us, Ellie looks the most like mom, so maybe Courtney's right. Maybe Ellie inherited some dislike of paranormal stuff."

"I don't *have* to have powers, do I?" Ellie's voice carried a bit of a panicky tone.

Angie took Ellie's hand and gave it a squeeze. "Mom didn't do anything with her powers, so you don't have to either. I don't think you have to worry."

Euclid and the black cat walked into the room and lay down on the rug in front of the fireplace.

"What about this cat?" Jenna asked.

"She hasn't asked to leave yet." Courtney went over to the cats and scratched them behind their ears. "I think we should keep her."

"I'll put an ad in the Sweet Cove weekly saying we found a cat," Angie said. "If the owner doesn't come forward, then I guess she'll stay."

"It's like Euclid was expecting her." Courtney patted the black cat's back. The animal purred.

Ellie's face took on a worried expression. "How would

Euclid know her? How would he know she was going to show up here?"

"Euclid knows everything," Courtney said. The orange cat rubbed his chin against Courtney's fingers. "He is a very smart boy."

The conversation turned to Mr. Finch's murder and his strange brother, who was still a guest in their B and B.

"What do you think of *our* Mr. Finch?" Jenna asked her sisters.

Angie passed the popcorn to Ellie. "Please don't call him *our* Mr. Finch. It sounds like we're going to be stuck with him."

"That wouldn't be so bad actually." Ellie dug into the bowl. "Having a permanent boarder would be good for us financially."

Courtney stretched out on the floor next to the cats. "I'm suspicious of him still. How did he show up on the day his brother gets killed? It's too much of a coincidence. After fifty years of not being in contact? How is that possible?"

Jenna looked off into space. "Wait." She sat up. "What if this Mr. Finch has powers?"

"What?" Ellie almost shrieked.

"Maybe he can sense things." Jenna was excited by her idea. "That's how he showed up in Sweet Cove. He sensed his brother was in danger."

Courtney pushed herself into sitting position. "Wow. That makes perfect sense."

"Only to a crazy person." Ellie harrumphed and shook her head. "What's happening to this family?"

"I wonder if he would open up to us. Maybe the chief makes him nervous." Angie reached for her iced tea. "We should have a casual conversation with him."

"I think he's avoiding telling anything important." Jenna put her feet up on the coffee table. "He talks, he answers questions, but there's never anything of substance to what he says. He's being deliberately evasive."

Courtney sprang up off the floor. "Angie. Your baking."

"What?" Angie blinked.

"Your baking. Some people say there's something special about your bakery items. They make them feel good. When the bake shop was open, some people only wanted you to make their drinks and only ate what you baked."

"That was just silly," Angie protested. "What does that have to do with Mr. Finch?"

"You should bake something. Get him to eat it. Maybe you could try to make the food item like a truth serum." Courtney sat down in the chair next to Angie and leaned forward.

"I don't get it," Jenna said.

"Angie is always happy and pleasant. She must somehow put those emotions into what she bakes. People feel good after they eat her baked goods." Courtney stared at each of her sisters. "This is Angie's power."

Euclid lifted his head.

"Oh God," Ellie groaned.

"Bake something," Courtney said. "Try to put the desire for truth into the item."

Angie's face was blank. "How would I do that?"

"I don't know. Just think about it while you make it." Courtney stood up. "Come on. Try it."

Angie started to protest. "I don't know. It sounds crazy."

"Exactly." Ellie frowned.

Jenna stood up. "It can't hurt to try it. Think of it as an experiment. Test what you're capable of." She grabbed Angie's hands and pulled her up from her seat. "It could be fun." Jenna laughed as she and Courtney corralled Angie and herded her into the kitchen.

Standing at the kitchen counter, Angie asked, "What should I make?" She was still wary about the idea.

"What does Mr. Finch like?" Courtney turned to Ellie. "Does he eat the same thing each morning?"

"He hasn't been here that long." Ellie thought about it and her eyes brightened. "He's had a muffin every morning. Blueberry." She shook her head and muttered. "Why am I helping with this?"

Everyone, but Ellie, bustled about the kitchen pulling out muffin tins, flour, eggs, and sugar. The ingredients were piled on the counter for Angie.

"How should I do it?" Angie put an apron over her head and tied it in back.

"Try thinking about what you want to happen." Courtney placed a big bowl in front of Angie.

Jenna carried the mixer to the table. "While preparing the batter, you should have purpose and intention about what you want from the muffins."

"This is ridiculous. It's stupid." Ellie rolled her eyes. "How can Angie put intention into a food product?"

Angie ignored her sister's comments and looked over all of the items. "Hmmm, okay." She picked up a measuring cup.

"Maybe close your eyes. To block out distractions," Courtney suggested.

Angie tilted her head to the side and gave her sister a

look. "Close my eyes? Then how will I bake if I can't see what I'm doing?"

Ellie stood up from the chair she'd been sitting in. "Maybe it's best if we clear out of here and let you work."

They all knew that Ellie didn't want to be part of the experiment and the reason for leaving the room had nothing to do with what was best for Angie's baking.

Jenna gave Ellie an empathetic smile and took her by the elbow. She steered her to the doorway. "You're probably right. We should let Angie do her thing. We shouldn't distract her. Let's leave her alone."

Courtney looked disappointed, but she followed Jenna's lead. "Okay. Good luck, Angie. Just focus on what you want the muffins to do." She gave Angie a hug and left the room.

Angie stared at the ingredients and the equipment. She wasn't sure what to do. It seemed an impossible task.

Euclid and the black cat entered the kitchen. Euclid led the way to the top of the refrigerator and his friend followed him. Angie looked at them. "I'm glad you're here, you two. You can keep me company. And bring me good luck."

She took a deep breath and plunged in to make her muffins. At first, Angie thought about Mr. Finch and getting him to tell the truth, but as she mixed, her mind wandered to other things. Josh Williams was a prominent part of her daydreams.

When she was finished, she placed the muffin mixture in the refrigerator for morning baking and started the kitchen clean up.

* * *

In the morning, Ellie eyed the muffin batter in the fridge with trepidation. She took a deep breath and reluctantly filled the tins. With trembling hands, she placed the tins in the oven, set the timer, and then prepared the other breakfast foods for the guests.

She carried the items to the buffet table in the dining room and placed the basket of muffins next to the bowl of mixed fruit. Spread across the top of the buffet, there were different selections of cereals in glass containers, a basket with bananas and apples, a bowl of yogurt, and several jugs filled with a variety of juices.

Besides Mr. Finch and Mr. and Mrs. Foley, the retired couple who was staying for two weeks, two elderly sisters had arrived the prior evening. Ellie was pleased with the reservations that had been coming in. The B and B would be nearly full every week during July and August, and September was filling fast.

As Ellie was bringing a pot of fresh coffee to the table, Mr. Finch appeared at the bottom of the staircase. He and Ellie exchanged greetings and Finch limped to his seat at the table.

"Would you like your usual, this morning, Mr. Finch?" Ellie filled his teacup.

"Maybe something different today."

Ellie's face blanched worried that Finch might not choose a muffin. It was her job to get him to eat one. "What can I get you?"

"I'd like a boiled egg and some wheat toast, please." Finch

went back to his paper and Ellie's heart sank as she walked to the kitchen to get the egg and toast.

Bringing the food back to the dining room, Ellie racked her brain for ideas to get Finch to eat a blueberry muffin. She heard the voices of the retired couple talking with Finch.

"Oh, Ellie, I was just telling Mr. Finch how delicious these muffins are." Mrs. Foley had two of the blueberry muffins on her plate slathered with butter.

Ellie wanted to hug Mrs. Foley. "They're one of Angie's specialties." She eyed Finch to see if he might go to the buffet table to get one, but Mr. Foley was conversing with him. Ellie wished Foley would just eat his breakfast and stop distracting Finch.

"Can I bring you a muffin, Mr. Finch?" Ellie plastered a pleasant smile on her face.

"What?" The old man glanced up. "Oh, yes. A muffin, please."

Ellie chose the largest one, placed it on a plate, and served it to Finch. Bustling about the room, Ellie's heart leaped with joy when she saw Finch bite into the muffin.

"Very good," he mumbled as he chewed.

Angie came down the stairs and said good morning to the guests. She chose fruit and yogurt from the buffet table and sat down across from Mr. Finch. He stared at her.

Angie could feel the man's eyes on her, and she took a quick look at him to see if something was wrong.

"Your muffins are…." Finch stopped in mid-sentence. "You look very beautiful this morning, Angie."

Angie was reaching for the creamer but her hand froze at Finch's comment. "Ah, thank you."

"You are an extraordinary woman, my dear. Why has no man snatched you up?"

Angie looked at Finch with wide eyes. Mr. and Mrs. Foley glanced at the older man out of the corner of their eyes. Ellie whirled towards Finch with her jaw hanging open.

"Just look at this woman." Finch leaned across the table, his eyes on Angie like lasers. "The porcelain skin, those eyes as blue as the ocean, and that figure…." Finch leered at Angie.

"Are you quite all right, Mr. Finch?" Mrs. Foley asked.

Dear God. What did that muffin do to him? Angie got up so fast from the table that her chair almost tipped over. She made eye contact with Ellie, who shrugged her shoulders.

"Well, I'm off for the day," Angie announced with mock cheerfulness. Eager to get away from Finch, she left her barely touched breakfast on the table and headed for the hallway that led to the kitchen.

"May I join you, my dear?" Finch asked hopefully.

"I'm afraid not." Angie hurried away. *What have I done?*

"Before you go, what about joining me upstairs in my room?" Mr. Finch cocked his head to one side and raised an eyebrow.

"Mr. Finch!" Mrs. Foley was appalled. She turned to Ellie. "Should we call an ambulance?"

"What?" Ellie watched Angie tear down the hallway. "Why?"

"Perhaps Mr. Finch has had a stroke." Mrs. Foley's face was pinched with worry.

"Nonsense, woman. I'm fit as a fiddle." Finch rose from his chair and limped for the hall calling to Angie.

"Mr. Finch." Ellie spoke harshly. "The kitchen area is off limits to guests."

"Well, an exception could be made in this case?" Finch smiled at Ellie.

"Absolutely not." Ellie brushed past the man. She carried an empty coffee pot to the kitchen to refill it. "Return to your seat."

Angie was about to leave through the back door off the kitchen when Ellie rushed in and asked, "What on earth is happening?"

"I have no idea." Angie's face was pale.

"How did this go wrong?" Ellie pulled her blonde ponytail over her shoulder and fiddled with the long strands. "What were you thinking about while you prepared the muffin batter?"

"About Finch telling the truth about things."

"Was that all? Did you keep your mind on that topic the whole time?"

Angie sat down in one of the kitchen chairs. "Mostly."

Ellie put her hands on her hips. She was afraid to ask, but said, "What else did you think about?"

Angie met Ellie's eyes. "Josh."

Ellie's hand flew to her mouth. "Oh, no. Finch has fallen in love with you. Your thoughts about Josh must have been so strong that they overrode your other intention to make Finch tell the truth."

Angie leaped from her seat. "How long is this going to last? It can't last forever, can it? How long will it take to wear off?" She stared with wild eyes towards the hall. "Go in there. Make him throw up."

"How?" Ellie's hands trembled when she brushed her hair back.

"Angie." Finch called from the dining room.

Angie grabbed her wallet from the counter and hurried to the back door. "I'm getting out of here. Text me when it's safe to come back."

"What should I do with him?" Ellie asked.

"Wake up Courtney. Tell her to think of something," Angie said over her shoulder.

"What if nothing works?" Ellie asked.

"Then we'll have to kill him." Angie opened the back door. She glanced back to see Ellie's horrified face. "Ellie, I'm kidding."

Ellie nodded. "Okay. Go." She turned her head to be sure Finch wasn't coming into the room. "It's best if he isn't around you right now. We'll think of something."

She hoped.

9

Angie hurried around the side of the Victorian being sure to hug the property line to keep as far from the house's windows as possible. She did not want Mr. Finch to see her escaping. She halted when she came up parallel with the front of the house and peeked around to see if anyone was on the porch. The coast was clear, so she rushed to the sidewalk and practically ran up Beach Street. Her mind was a jumble. Angie felt awful that she tried to manipulate Mr. Finch into being forthcoming about his relationship with his murdered brother by concocting a "truth" muffin. She never dreamed that the experiment would backfire in such a weird way. *Please let his mood be temporary.*

Angie kept looking over her shoulder to be sure that Finch wasn't following behind. When she reached the main street of Sweet Cove, Angie thought she might try to pass a few hours by walking down to Robin's Point. She could hang around near the cove to browse the stores, walk along the beach, and get some lunch because if she didn't keep herself busy, she'd go crazy from worrying about what was going on back at the Victorian.

Angie had no idea how long the muffin "spell" would last, but its duration would dictate the length of time she would need to stay away from the house. She checked her phone for any messages from her sisters. *Nothing.*

Wiping nervous perspiration from her brow, she decided to duck into the small grocery store on Main Street for a bottle of water. Approaching the checkout counter with her purchase, she greeted the store owner. He was talking with a Sweet Cove cab driver who Angie knew. Walt, the cab driver, had often picked up Angie or her sisters at the train station and driven them into town.

"Hey, Angie." Walt put his coffee cup down on the end of the checkout counter. "How are you? I heard you found old Finch's body."

She nodded as she pulled money from her pocket to pay for her purchase. "Courtney and I found him."

"That must have been a shock."

The store owner rang the sale into the cash register.

"And so soon after Professor Linden was murdered." Walt stroked his chin. "What's going on in this town? Did someone put a spell on our pretty, little Sweet Cove?"

At his mention of the word *spell*, Angie shot Walt a horrified look.

"Did Finch have any relatives, I wonder?" The owner handed Angie her change.

She put the money in her pocket and picked up the bottle of water. "Finch had a brother. In fact, he's a guest at the Victorian. He checked into the B and B the day Finch was killed."

"He had a brother?" the store owner asked. "I never saw Finch with anyone."

"The brother lives on the west coast. He arrived in town on the day of the murder." Angie found a hair elastic in her pocket and, balancing the water under her arm, she pulled her honey colored locks into a high ponytail.

"The brother was here before the day of the murder." Walt took a sip of his coffee.

Angie cocked her head to the side. "He was?"

"Yeah." Walt swirled his coffee around in the paper cup. "I picked him up at the train station a couple of days before Finch got killed."

"I thought he arrived the very day of the murder." Angie's brows drew together.

"Nope."

"You're sure it was Finch's brother? Did he introduce himself to you?"

"No, but I recognized him getting into the police car at your house the other day. I was driving by. That's the brother, right?"

Angie nodded. "We were all going with Chief Martin to Finch's house."

"The brother has a house here?" the store owner asked.

"No," Angie said. "We were going to dead Finch's house." She turned to Walt. "Are you sure you picked him up before the day of the murder?"

"I know I'm getting old, Angie, but I'm not senile yet." Walt chuckled.

"Where did you drop him off?"

"At the resort." Walt drained his cup. "Gotta go. Can't be hanging around shooting the breeze all day." He threw his cup in the trash can behind the counter and strode out the door.

Angie left the store right after Walt, her mind puzzling over why Finch might have told her that he only came to town on the day of the murder when Walt said he dropped Finch at the resort two days prior. She turned left and headed down the street towards Robin's Point.

* * *

Angie walked onto the grounds of the resort. She could feel the familiar humming in her blood that happened whenever she was on the point. Years ago, her grandmother had owned a cottage on Robin's Point where Angie and her sisters spent many happy weeks. Being on the point always caused a low level pulsing in Angie's blood. Courtney told her that she could feel the thrumming too and that it made her feel close to Nana.

Angie walked into the lobby of the resort and went to speak with one of the registration clerks on duty.

"Could you tell me if Mr. Victor Finch has been a recent guest here?" Angie questioned.

"I'm sorry, but we aren't allowed to give out information on guests."

Angie sighed. She should have thought of that. Privacy

laws would forbid such information being shared with the public. She would have to speak to Chief Martin and let him know that Finch was in town a couple of days before the murder took place. "Thank you, anyway." She stepped away from the counter and headed for the front door. She checked her phone for messages with any updates on Mr. Finch's condition, but there was nothing. Angie's stomach clenched with anxiety. She worried that she might have put a permanent spell on the older man.

Wondering how to reverse what she'd done to Finch, she walked outside and crossed the lawn of the resort to go and sit where her grandmother's cottage used to be. She stretched out on the grass and watched the waves crashing against the rocks. She could see people strolling on the beach below the point. Some brave souls were jumping around in the icy waves. Angie nearly shivered thinking about how cold the ocean water would be this early in the season.

Her mind puzzled over the two Finch brothers and their estrangement. She couldn't fathom bearing a grudge so great that it kept her away from her sisters for over fifty years. Pondering who could have killed Finch and why, Angie rested back on the sun-warmed lawn and looked up at the bright blue of the sky. She closed her eyes and was lulled by the gentle thrumming moving through her veins. It only took a few minutes for her to fall asleep.

* * *

Angie sat bolt upright and gaped at her surroundings trying to get her bearings. She blinked from the glaring sunlight and put her hand up to shield her eyes. Remembering why she'd left the Victorian, apprehension gripped her. She rubbed her forehead for a minute, and then stood up, brushing the grass from her butt.

"Angie!" Josh Williams called to her from across the lawn. "What a nice surprise." He grinned. "I never know where you're going to turn up."

Josh's smile sent warm shivers across Angie's skin.

"I took some time off from helping Ellie with the B and B. It's so nice out. I felt like a long walk to get some exercise. I ended up here." Angie gave Josh a sheepish grin. "I fell asleep."

"Well, it's no wonder." Josh stepped closer. "You've been working so hard with the bake shop closing and the bed and breakfast starting up. Not to mention everything that happened surrounding Professor Linden's murder."

Angie sighed. "You heard about the candy shop owner? Mr. Finch was killed."

Josh nodded. "That was a terrible shock."

"Did you hear Courtney and I found him?"

Josh's eyes widened. "What? You found him? Angie, I'm so sorry."

Angie loved the sincerity and caring in Josh's voice.

"Listen, do you have to get back right away? Can you have lunch with me? We've both been so busy. It would be nice to just sit and talk."

Angie's long lashes fluttered over her blue eyes. "I'd like that." She looked down at her jeans. "I'm not dressed for the restaurant though."

"The restaurant doesn't open until later in the afternoon. We can eat lunch in the café."

Josh and Angie went into the resort's cafe and took a table by the windows looking over the Atlantic Ocean.

"How are things here? Have you cleared up the issues with the manager?" Angie sipped her ice water.

Josh leaned forward and lowered his voice. "I don't know. He talks a good game, but I'm not sure about him. He seems ... distracted. He does unexpected things. He was out of touch with the resort for an entire day. No one knew where he was. He was supposed to be here. The assistant manager tried to call him, but he never picked up. He showed up the next day. Never gave a reason for his absence. I've discussed it with him, what our expectations are. There have been other things, too. Nothing is enough to remove him from the position, but if it keeps up, we might not have a choice."

"He came well-recommended?"

"Yes, highly. But the guy working for us doesn't seem like the one with the great recommendations and resume." Josh looked across the room and nodded. "That's him speaking with the hostess."

Angie glanced over. A tall, slender, man dressed in what appeared to be an expensive suit stood next to the hostess going over some papers. The man was middle-aged with dark brown hair. Some gray showed at his temples. "He looks very professional and polished."

"His name is Andrew Flynn. He's worked all over the world. Davis and I thought we hit the jackpot getting a guy like this to run the resort. Now I'm not so sure."

Their meals arrived and the subject changed to other things. Angie enjoyed spending an hour with Josh. It almost made her forget why she had left the Victorian. Just as that thought entered her mind, her phone buzzed.

"Go ahead," Josh said. "Check it."

Angie lifted the phone from her pocket and looked at the text. *Come home.*

"I need to get back." Nervous tension made Angie's heart pound. She wished her sister had sent a little more information than only a two word text.

10

Angie jogged the miles from the point to the center of Sweet Cove and she slowed to a walk as she turned on to Beach Street. Her leg muscles were tight and her lungs burned. She realized she needed to get more regular exercise.

By the time she climbed the Victorian's front porch steps, her breathing continued to be quick and labored, but now the reason wasn't because she had been running. Angie didn't know what awaited her inside the house. Twice on her way home, she'd stopped and texted Ellie and Courtney, but neither one replied. Her heart hammered. Her stomach clenched with worry as she reached for the doorknob, turned it slowly, and tip-toed into the foyer.

Angie looked into the living room and her heart jumped into her throat when saw Mr. Finch sprawled on the sofa.

Her hand flew up to her mouth to stifle a gasp. A blanket haphazardly covered Finch and a cold compress lay across his forehead. What Angie could see of his face was ghostly pale. His eyes were closed. She thought he looked like he was dead.

Euclid and the black cat were perched on the back of the sofa watching over Finch.

The soft click of shoes on the wood floor caused Angie to turn towards the hall. Ellie came into the foyer carrying a tray with a glass of water and a cup of tea on it. She put an index finger to her lips indicating the need for quiet.

Angie nodded.

Ellie went into the living room and placed the tray on the coffee table. She went back into the foyer and took Angie by the elbow steering her down the hallway and into the family room at the back of the house.

"What's been happening?" Angie asked. "How's Mr. Finch?"

Ellie sat down on the comfy sofa. "He seems fine now. I think the spell or whatever it was is over."

Angie blew out a sigh of relief.

"He wanted to search the house for you. Courtney came down and corralled him in the living room. She told him you would be angry if he didn't behave."

The corners of Angie's mouth turned up and she couldn't keep herself from chuckling.

Ellie frowned. "Yes. Laugh. I was a nervous wreck." She pulled her long blonde hair over her shoulder. "After three hours of his foolishness, he suddenly got a headache and collapsed on the sofa. Courtney and Jenna stayed with him. He fell asleep, but had wild dreams. He was calling out, thrashing."

"Oh, no." Angie felt awful for causing Finch's ordeal.

"At last, he calmed. He's been quiet. I think he'll be okay when he wakes up." Ellie shook her head. "Our poor guests, the Foleys. Mrs. Foley wanted to call an ambulance. She was sure Finch had lost his mind, or he'd had a stroke. I made up a story that Finch had a strong reaction to a new medication."

"What clever thinking. You handled the whole mess perfectly." Angie praised her sister. "Where are Jenna and Courtney?"

"They're in Jenna's shop working on the jewelry."

Euclid and the black cat appeared at the entrance to the family room. Euclid let out a howl. Ellie and Angie jumped.

"Finch must be awake. Euclid and the other cat have been watching over him." Ellie stood up and headed for the living room with Angie following behind. Ellie said over her shoulder, "We need to name that cat. And why is she always trying to get into my office?"

"Is she? I didn't know."

"She meows at the door until I let her in there," Ellie said. "She's obsessed with that room."

They approached the living room.

Mr. Finch was sitting up on the sofa rubbing his fore-head. A lock of his gray hair hung over his face. He lifted his tired eyes as the girls and the cats hurried towards him. Making eye contact with Finch, a quiver of worry shuddered down Angie's spine that maybe the spell hadn't let go of him, but his voice was soft and his facial expression remained flat when he saw her. Angie let out the breath she had been holding tight in her lungs.

"How are you feeling, Mr. Finch?" Angie wondered if Finch would remember the feelings he had experienced for her.

"I had a headache. It came on quickly." He reached for the glass of water.

"Can we get you anything?" Ellie sat down in the chair next to the sofa.

Finch gulped his water and set the glass back on the tray. "I think I'd like to go up to my room. Perhaps take a shower." He glanced around looking for his cane.

Angie spotted the cane partially hidden under the sofa. She bent and lifted it off the floor. She passed it to Mr. Finch and as they both held on to it, a wave of dizziness washed over her. Angie sucked in a short, quick gasp. Her vision darkened until she could only see through a small hole.

She pictured herself standing at the top of a long staircase. A man's voice shouted, but the sound was muffled. The anger in the voice was directed at her. Adrenaline pulsed through her veins. The voice shouted again, closer this time. Someone came at her. His hands clutched her neck and pushed her backwards. In slow motion, she plunged down the staircase, her spine cracking against each tread of the stairs. Pain flashed in her back until it consumed her.

In the void, a tiny pin prick sparkled and expanded until Angie's vision fully returned. A breath of air escaped her throat. She released her hold on Mr. Finch's cane.

"Are you okay?" Ellie gave her sister a strange look.

"I think I'm getting a headache. I felt dizzy for a second." Angie took a quick look at Mr. Finch.

He pushed himself off the sofa, holding tight to his cane. Ellie took Finch's arm and the two walked to the front staircase.

"Be careful on the stairs," Angie called to them as Ellie helped Mr. Finch up to his room.

* * *

The four sisters sat on the sofas in the family room each holding plates with slices of pizza and portions of fresh salad. Angie made the pizza after she'd had a nap and a shower. She wanted to cook something normal, something that no one would have a weird reaction to. She was careful not to put any intentions into the dough.

"Next time you attempt a spell, you need to keep focused on your thoughts." Courtney bit into her pizza slice. "Don't let extraneous ideas surface while you bake."

"I didn't realize," Angie said. "At least now we know that things wear off, it's nothing permanent. Thankfully."

Jenna said, "Still, you'll need to be careful when you bake. Make sure nothing slips from your mind into the food."

"I'm just glad Mr. Finch is okay." Ellie grabbed a napkin from the coffee table.

Angie told her sisters what the cab driver said about Finch arriving in Sweet Cove two days prior to the murder. "I distinctly remember Finch telling me that he'd only just arrived on the morning of the murder."

Courtney sat up. "Why did he lie? Did he kill his brother?"

Jenna looked at Ellie. "You clean his room everyday. Look through his things. See if you can find any evidence. Maybe he has a shirt with blood on it."

"I'm not looking through his things." Ellie stabbed a piece of lettuce with her fork. "That's completely unethical."

"So is murdering your brother," Jenna said. Her legs were curled under her, the dinner plate balanced on her knees.

"Something happened to me when I passed Finch his cane today." Angie told them of the vision she had of being shoved down a staircase.

"What was that about?" Ellie's face had worry lines creased across her forehead.

"Was it a warning?" Jenna turned concerned eyes to Angie. "A premonition?"

Angie shrugged. "I don't know. I'll just be careful around stairs for a while, I guess."

"Wait." Courtney's eyes widened. "Was Finch holding the cane at the same time you held it?"

"I think so," Angie said. "Yes, I handed it to him, so we both had our hands on it at the same time. Why?"

"Could the vision have been from Finch? Like a memory, transmitted to you through the cane?" Courtney said.

The three girls' faces were blank. They thought about Courtney's idea.

"Maybe?" Angie said with a soft voice.

Jenna said, "Maybe the image crossed into your mind because Finch had recently been under your muffin spell."

"Why does everyone have powers surfacing all of a sudden?" Ellie looked like she had eaten something bad. "Is it this house?" She glanced around the room, a worried and frightened look on her face.

"I don't have any powers." Even though Jenna was trying to reassure her sister, she sounded slightly disappointed in her lack of abilities.

"It's not the house," Courtney said. "It's us." She reached for another slice of pizza.

Ellie put her empty plate on the coffee table. "Why don't you just ask Finch again if he was in town prior to the day his bother was killed? Maybe it's just a misunderstanding." Ellie picked up her glass of lemon water. "And then you could ask him, oh by the way, have you ever been pushed down a flight of stairs?"

"He might find that an odd question." Angie smiled. "I think I'm done pestering Mr. Finch."

Angie's phone buzzed with an incoming call.

Euclid let out a hiss.

Angie didn't recognize the number, but answered anyway. "Hello?" She listened for a few seconds and then bolted up off the sofa with the phone still pressed to her ear. "Okay. We'll see you in a few minutes. Thanks." She ended the call. "That was Chief Martin." Angie let the hand holding the phone fall to her side. "The artwork at the late Mr. Finch's house…one of the paintings has been stolen."

"What?!" The three girls howled.

"The chief is coming over in a few minutes to tell Mr. Finch."

11

Angie ushered the chief into the living room where Mr. Finch sat waiting for him. Ellie had been sitting with Finch keeping him company and she stood when Chief Martin entered the room. Angie and Ellie thought it best if the two men spoke in private so they started to walk away, but Finch asked them to remain in the living room with him.

"It would be helpful to me if you listened to what Chief Martin has to tell me. I'd like to be able to talk things over with someone, so I'd like you to hear the details first hand."

When everyone was settled in their seats, the chief cleared his throat. "I'm sorry to report that your brother's house was broken into. It seems to have been a purposeful robbery. The largest painting was taken. Nothing else appeared to have been removed from the house."

"That's no surprise. That painting was the most valuable." Finch gripped the top of his cane with both hands.

"The break-in occurred in the last three days. We've had patrol cars driving by the house periodically and an officer inspects the outside of the property every other day. This afternoon one of the officers walked around the premises and noticed the back door ajar. He investigated and discovered the painting missing." The chief let out a long sigh.

Angie asked, "What about the burglar alarm. You set it when we left the house the other day."

"It had been disarmed."

"Obviously someone knew the painting was in the house … and that there was an alarm." Ellie's forehead was creased.

"That information was never publicized, was it?" Angie looked at the chief. "That the late Mr. Finch had valuable artwork in his house?"

"No." The chief shook his head. "If that was made known, it would be an open invitation to thieves."

"Perhaps," Finch's voice shook, "my brother's killer came back and took the painting?"

Chief Martin lifted his hands, the palms up. "That is unknown at this time. It can't be ruled out, I'm afraid. It's a possibility."

Angie glanced at Mr. Finch. His facial muscles were slack and his wrinkles looked more pronounced. The murder and the break-in were taking a toll on him. Her attempt at the muffin "spell" hadn't done him any good either.

The chief spoke again. "Our concern is about the other paintings in the house. We think they should be removed. I spoke with the bank in town. They don't have the means to protect or store the artwork. We could keep the paintings at the police station for a short time. My recommendation to you, Mr. Finch, would be to retain an attorney to help you navigate the legal mess of your brother's estate. An attorney could start the proceedings for you to take over the belongings, the house, the candy store, and any other of your brother's holdings, and he or she could advise you on how best to protect the remaining paintings. In the meantime, we can remove the artwork to the police station, with your permission, of course. We can hold them there until you make other arrangements."

Mr. Finch nodded.

"Would you like me to contact the town attorney? Ask him to get in touch with you?" Chief Martin asked. "His name is Jack Ford."

Angie and Ellie exchanged worried looks at the mention of the lawyer.

"Please do." Mr. Finch said.

The chief finished up with Mr. Finch and he left the house. Angie and Ellie stayed in the living room in case Finch wanted to talk.

"I'm sorry about the painting," Ellie said.

Finch tried to force a slight smile. "It was never mine anyway."

Euclid and the black cat jumped up beside Finch and he patted them absent-mindedly. When the purring started, Finch smiled. "Such a comforting sound. You are both very fine animals."

"Be careful with your praise, Mr. Finch," Ellie told him. "It goes straight to Euclid's head."

"And, what about the other cat?" He scratched the black cat's cheek. "Does praise go to her head, as well?"

Angie said, "We don't know her well enough to say."

Ellie looked at Angie. "No one answered the ad you placed for her."

"I guess she is the newest member of your family then." Mr. Finch looked kindly at the dark feline. "You'll be needing a name."

Courtney and Jenna came in and sat with the others. They heard what Finch said.

"Do you have a suggestion?" Jenna asked him.

The older man stroked the cat's luxurious ebony fur. "What about Circe?"

"What a pretty name." Courtney smiled. "How did you think of it?"

"It's from Greek mythology. Circe was the goddess of magic." Mr. Finch rested his cane against the arm of the sofa.

"I think it's perfect," Courtney said.

Euclid sat up and trilled.

Everyone chuckled.

Angie looked over at the orange cat. "I guess you approve, Euclid."

"Then Circe it is," Jenna agreed.

* * *

Angie was up late sitting at the dining room table going over Tom's estimate for the Victorian's renovations. She used a pencil to write her questions in the margin of the report. Her sisters had gone to bed over an hour ago. Euclid slept on top of the cabinet. Circe meowed from the hallway. She sat at the door to the den and Angie got up to open it for her.

"What's so great about this den? There are seventeen other rooms you can go into, you know."

Angie had just returned to her seat at the dining table when she heard soft footsteps on the stairs. Mr. Finch was coming down the steps dressed in his pajamas, robe, and slippers.

"Can't you sleep, Mr. Finch?" Angie placed the pencil on the table.

"I didn't think anyone was still up." Finch took slow steps into the dining room. "I sometimes have trouble falling asleep. The events of the past week haven't helped in that regard." He gave Angie a weary smile.

Euclid lifted his head, saw it was Finch, and went back to sleep.

Each night, Ellie left hot water, coffee, juice, and ice water on the side board for the guests. There was a basket of fresh fruit, a hazelnut cake, and a glass domed platter with chocolate-brownie cookies and biscuits.

Mr. Finch poured himself a glass of water. "May I sit here with you?"

"Of course. I'm just reviewing the estimate for the renovations."

"When will they start working on the house?" Finch sipped his water.

"Not until I have the deed. Probably in a couple of months."

Finch took another sip, and then placed the glass on the table. He raised his eyes to Angie. There were heavy bags under his eyes which pulled the lower lids down slightly. His pale blue eyes looked watery and a tiny bit red.

His voice was calm when he asked, "Do you want to ask me something?"

Angie was about to dismiss Finch's idea that she might have a question for him, but she changed her mind and decided not to deny it. The corners of her mouth turned up and she tipped her head to the side. "How do you know that I have a question?"

Finch said simply, "It's written on your face."

Angie folded her arms and leaned on the table. "I was at the market this morning. One of the town cab drivers was there. He told me that he picked you up at the train station two days before your brother's murder."

"Ah, I see." He nodded his head slightly. "But what is your question?"

"Were you in Sweet Cove two days before the murder?"

His answer was straight-forward. "Yes,"

"But you told me you had just arrived in town the morning that your brother died."

"I had."

Confusion furrowed Angie's brow. She tipped her head forward keeping eye contact with the older man. She waited for Finch to clarify.

"I arrived in Sweet Cove by train and a cab took me to the resort. I ate lunch there. Then a cab took me to Marblehead where I stayed for two nights."

"Why did you go to Marblehead?"

"I wasn't ready to see my brother. I didn't want to stay in Sweet Cove because I didn't want to run into him. It took me a couple of days to pluck up my courage."

"Was that because you hadn't seen him for such a long time?"

"That, yes. But for other reasons."

Angie's mind raced. *Does he mean he needed time to gather the courage to kill his brother?* "Then what happened?"

"I thought I might just leave the area and return to California without making contact with Thaddeus, but then I berated myself for being so foolish. I had come all this way. I made up my mind that I would leave Marblehead and return to Sweet Cove so I called and made the reservations to stay here at the B and B. Then I decided to go to the candy store."

"Did your brother know you were in town?"

Finch shook his head vigorously. "No."

Angie said, "And when you arrived at the candy store…?"

"I found out my brother was dead."

Angie said, "I don't mean this to sound disrespectful … but it didn't seem like you were upset."

"I was shocked. To think, the very day I came to see him, my brother is killed. It's been fifty years. I didn't know him anymore. He was someone from my past. I felt sadness, but not grief."

Angie sighed. It made sense. "Why did you decide to seek out your brother now, after so many years had passed?"

"Because. We're old." He touched his index finger to the water glass and traced along the side. "My brother wasn't a nice person."

Angie's eyebrows went up. She was surprised to hear this from Finch. She'd assumed that the candy store owner had soured over time … that some disappointments or upsets had changed who he was, slowly, the way wind and rain wear down the side of a cliff. But here was Finch reporting that his brother hadn't been a nice person from the very beginning.

"Not only was he not a nice person, he was mean," Finch

said. "He could be cruel. And, selfish."

Angie's heart felt heavy.

Finch put his hands in his lap and leaned against the chair back. He was quiet for several moments. Angie thought he must be reflecting on the past.

Finch looked across the table at Angie. "You handed me my cane earlier this afternoon."

Angie sat up straight. Adrenaline pumped through her veins. "Yes." Her voice was small as she recalled the vision.

Finch scrutinized Angie, and then seemed to make a decision. "I fell down a staircase, a long time ago. The fall almost killed me." He glanced at his cane which leaned against the chair next to him. "That's the reason I use the cane. People think it's because I'm an old man, but I've had to use it for over fifty years."

Over fifty years. The same amount of time that Finch had been estranged from his brother. A chill trickled down Angie's back.

Finch lowered his gaze to his hands. "My brother … Thaddeus … he pushed me down the stairs. He tried to kill me."

12

When Angie realized her mouth was hanging open, she snapped it shut. "He pushed you? It was intentional?"

"Yes." Finch's facial muscles drooped and his skin was tinged with a gray pallor as if the blood had drained away.

Angie couldn't believe this awful news. "Why? Why would he do such a terrible thing? He was your brother."

Finch looked across the room at nothing. A heaviness seemed to settle over him causing his head to hang forward and his shoulders to sag. At last he spoke. "My brother was a miserable person. I've spent a good deal of time reflecting on this. I believe he was born with a nasty temperament and it only got worse with time."

Circe came into the room from the hallway, crossed to where Finch sat, and leaped onto his lap where she settled.

"Oh," Finch said. The suddenness of the cat's action surprised him. He instinctively ran his hand over the soft fur and the feline purred.

Angie thought the cat sensed Finch's distress and offered comfort by snuggling on his lap. "Mr. Finch," Angie said gently. "Could I wake my sisters? I'd like them to be part of this conversation. It might give us some details that could help solve the murder."

"I don't mind if you do." His hand slid over the cat's black fur.

Angie roused the girls from their slumber and the three of them stumbled with sleepy eyes down to the dining room where they gathered around the table. Courtney couldn't suppress a yawn. She apologized.

Jenna blinked from the bright lights. "Angie told us that your brother pushed you on a staircase. Is it possible it was an accident?"

Finch's eyes flashed. "It was no accident."

Ellie pulled her robe around her. "Can you go on with your story, Mr. Finch? Can you tell us what happened?"

Finch gave a slight nod. "Thaddeus and I grew up in Chicago. I was the oldest by three years. He was often in trouble. He caused great turmoil in the house. My father died right after Thaddeus was born. My poor mother had a difficult time trying to raise my brother. I had a job in a factory. Thaddeus couldn't keep a job because of his temper. I wanted to help him … and to give our mother some peace of mind. She always worried about what would become of Thaddeus, and so I proposed a business deal with him."

"What sort of deal?" Courtney asked.

Finch said, "When I was in my twenties, our grandmother died. She left me her book of recipes. She'd been a baker and a confectioner in her native Sweden. I enjoyed trying out the recipes and working on them until they tasted like the ones Grandma made. I worked double shifts at the factory to save money to open a bakery and candy shop. When I wasn't at the factory, I worked on the recipes."

Jenna said, "You asked your brother to go into business with you?"

Finch nodded. "Thaddeus got into trouble with the police, for breaking and entering. He served a year in jail. I offered to teach him how to bake and make the candy. I told him that when he got out of prison, I would have enough saved to finance a business for the two of us."

"Did he agree to work with you?" Ellie asked.

"He did. He seemed excited about the possibility." Finch went quiet. He looked down at his hands and rubbed the skin of his wrists. Circe was still in his lap.

"What happened?" Angie watched Euclid sitting beside Finch's chair.

"I lived with our mother. She passed away two months before Thaddeus got out of jail. She left the house to us. We agreed to put the house up for sale and it sold quickly. The money was placed in the business account I'd set up at the bank under both of our names. I put all the money I'd saved in there as well." Finch swallowed. He made eye contact with the four girls. "You can guess what happened."

Courtney sat up, her blue eyes blazing. "Thaddeus stole the money?"

Finch's eyes misted over. "After the closing was complete with the new owners, I went to the house to pick up a few of my belongings, my grandmother's recipe book and a small painting she'd left me. When I entered the house, I heard a noise upstairs. I thought Thaddeus must have come to say goodbye to the house." Finch snorted. "I was such a fool.

I went up to the second floor. I called his name. He came out of my room. He was holding the recipe book and the painting."

Finch took a drink from his glass. "I've never told anyone this." He sucked in a breath and went on. "I asked Thaddeus what he was doing. His face twisted with rage. He told me he was taking the things. He hated me. He hated our mother. He charged at me and hit me in the chest. I fell. Backwards." A tear fell from his eye and plopped onto Circe's fur.

"How terrible," Ellie whispered.

Finch swallowed hard. "I was unconscious at the bottom of the stairs when the new owners came in late that night. I was in the hospital for a very long time. I discovered that my brother had emptied the bank account and had disappeared. I was penniless. I had no way to find him. I went to the police, but nothing ever came of it. He was gone."

"What did you do?" Courtney asked.

He gestured at his cane. "Because of my injury, I couldn't go back to work at the factory."

"So you became a teacher? You told us you'd been a math teacher." Angie shifted in her seat.

Euclid let out a small hiss.

Finch gave a half smile to the orange cat. "I believe Euclid is on to me. I only say that I was a teacher because it's easy for people to believe." He reached down and scratched Euclid's cheek. "However, it seems certain orange cats don't believe that story." Circe jumped down from the man's lap and sat beside Euclid. "I discovered that after my fall, I had a certain gift."

Ellie's eyes widened. She glanced at her sisters. "What kind of gift?" She braced for the answer.

"I sometimes could see things. Premonitions, if you will."

Ellie looked like she might faint.

Courtney leaned forward. "That's so cool."

"So I set up a business in my apartment. I gave readings to people."

"You can see the future?" Jenna asked.

"No. It's not like that. I get a small sense of people. It's only little things that I see or feel, nothing major or life-altering. People seem to like it though, that I know some slight thing about them."

Courtney had a thoughtful expression on her face. "I think everyone wants to be known to someone, however little the knowing is."

The four sisters sat in silence thinking over what they'd learned about the Mr. Finch sitting at their table and the dead Mr. Finch.

Jenna asked, "What was the painting that your grandmother gave you? That your brother stole from you?"

"It was an abstract, by a Swedish painter. Grandmother knew that I loved to draw. Any chance I got, I would spend hours painting and sketching. I've always loved colors and shapes."

"I wonder what happened to the painting." Ellie absent-mindedly twisted the long locks of her hair.

Finch said, "It's hanging on the wall of my brother's living room."

13

It was late when they finally went to bed. No one slept very soundly except for Finch. Angie thought that Mr. Finch seemed lighter after he revealed the details of his estrangement from his brother. She wondered if releasing the story from his mind had helped him in some way.

The alarms woke the four sisters early and none of them had much energy when they first arrived downstairs for breakfast. Mr. Finch, however, was bright and happy. Mr. and Mrs. Foley joined Finch at the dining room table and told him they were sorry he had been unwell the previous day and that they were pleased that he had made such a quick recovery. Angie whole-heartedly agreed with them.

Courtney pulled a gallon of milk from the refrigerator. "Can you imagine your own sibling hurting you like Mr. Finch's brother hurt him?"

"What a terrible, terrible man." Ellie was placing dishes in the dishwasher. "We knew he was an angry, miserable old thing, but I had no idea." She shook her head. "It's mind-boggling how cruel a person can be."

"I'd like to know who murdered dead Finch." Jenna sat at the kitchen table eating an egg and toast. "I'd like to know why."

"Finch must have been awful to plenty of people. There must be a life-time's worth of angry people. It could be any-one who killed him." Courtney poured milk into her cereal bowl. "It could be someone from his past come to get even with him."

Angie sipped from a mug. "I wish we could help fig-ure out who committed the crime. Even though dead Finch was a monster, people can't take things into their own hands. There's a killer on the loose around here."

"It won't do the town any good to have an unsolved murder." Ellie was scurrying around the kitchen. "This is supposed to be a lovely, peaceful place to live and vacation. Townspeople are on edge. The killer has to be caught."

Courtney tipped her cereal bowl to her lips to get the last of the milk. She set the bowl down on the floor and Circe and Euclid took turns licking up the last drops. "We should go talk to the candy store's other employees." She looked at Angie. "You and I are the only ones who don't have jobs now. Let's go see what we can learn about dead Finch."

"I'd be glad to assign you some tasks to do around here." Ellie glanced at her two sisters as she filled a basket with muf-fins.

Angie smiled. "I think solving the murder is a higher priority." She winked at Courtney. "Let's get ready."

Courtney didn't need to be asked twice. "I'll meet you at the front door in fifteen minutes."

Ellie stacked some clean plates on the counter. "Attorney Ford is coming by soon to drop off some paperwork about making the B and B an official business. It will help with taxes and insurance and liability. We can go over it later today. He's also meeting with Mr. Finch."

Angie did not want to see Attorney Ford. "Thanks for the warning."

She and Courtney made eye contact with each other.

"I'll meet you at the door in *five* minutes." Courtney hurried out of the kitchen with Angie right behind her.

* * *

The girls walked down Beach Street side by side. Puffy white clouds floated against the bright blue of the sky. The sun's rays announced the approach of the summer season.

Courtney said, "Let's go see Mr. Adams. He worked at Finch's candy store for about two months. After the murder, he got a job working the reception desk at the Blue Waves Inn on the beach."

Angie said, "Maybe he has some insight."

Courtney narrowed her eyes. "Maybe he killed Finch."

Angie chuckled. "I love how you never dismiss anyone as innocent until proven so."

"Hmmph." Courtney grunted. "I'm just careful. People can surprise you." She watched a blue truck drive up the street towards them. "There's Tom." She waved.

Angie waved too and looked over her shoulder. "He's stopping at the Victorian."

"He's doing a lot of that lately." Courtney gave an impish smile. "Whatever could be the attraction there?"

"Hmm." Angie stroked her chin pretending to ponder that question. "Could it be someone with long, light brown hair and blue eyes?"

"Someone who designs and makes jewelry? Could that be the reason Tom is drawn to the house?" Courtney smiled.

"It's possible." Angie's eyes sparkled. "Maybe we should question Tom about the reason he stops at the Victorian for coffee almost every day."

"We'll get to the bottom of it." Courtney snickered. "Just wait until Tom's doing the renovation work at the house. We can tease him about Jenna every day."

"I can't wait." Angie rubbed her hands together.

As they walked down the slight hill, the girls looked out over the wide, white sand beach of Sweet Cove. Some people were leaping in the waves, and others sunned themselves on blankets or in beach chairs. Children threw Frisbees and flew kites. A sailboat bobbed on the ocean.

Right before the beach, on the left side of the street, stood a small hotel, an inn, two restaurants, a convenience store, and a snack counter. A little kid sat on a bench in front of the stores swinging his tiny legs back and forth, licking an ice cream cone.

Angie wanted to join the little kid to sit in the sun and eat ice cream. "Want to sit for a few minutes before we go in? The sun feels good."

The girls took a seat on a bench near the beach. They watched the ocean waves and the people enjoying the sun.

"Tell me about Mr. Adams," Angie asked.

Courtney rolled up the sleeves of her shirt. The day was turning out to be warmer than expected. "Mr. Adams is retired. He's had a small house here in town for years. He moved in permanently after retiring from his job. He told me he likes to work part-time to get out, see people. He used to come to Finch's store for the three to nine at night shift. I sort of envied him because for the last two hours of his shift, Finch would leave the store for the day and go home. Mr. Adams would lock up. He had some peace for a couple of hours without Finch glaring at him and watching everything he did."

"That's what Finch was like when you worked there?"

"Oh, yeah. I wouldn't be surprised if Finch had security cameras trained on us so he could observe what we were doing in the front of the store while he was making the candy."

"It wasn't just you and Mr. Adams working at the store, right? He must have had other employees."

Courtney nodded. "Every summer Finch hired students from abroad to come and work there. They had summer work contracts otherwise I don't know how any of them would stay for four months working for him."

"Had they arrived yet?"

"Yes. Two of them had arrived. Mr. Adams was training them."

"So they weren't ever there alone with Finch?"

"Not yet. Finch had the Walsh sisters working there too."

"I forgot about the Walsh sisters." Angie's eyebrows went up. "They must be in their late eighties."

"Mr. Adams said the sisters had worked at the shop for about a year." Courtney rolled her eyes. "They must have won the prize for longest employment."

"Prize or punishment?" Angie pushed her honey colored hair back from her face. "How'd they stand him?"

"Who knows?" Courtney looked at Angie and raised an

eyebrow. "Maybe we should ask them."

Angie nodded. "They'll be next on our interrogation list."

The girls got up and walked over to the inn where Mr. Adams manned the front reception desk. When they entered the lobby, Adams was writing a note on a piece of paper. He heard the door open and looked up. Adams was thin, slight, and wiry. He was balding and wore black rimmed glasses. His bushy gray eyebrows tried to hide behind the rims of his glasses, but they stuck up over the tops like unruly bushes growing over a fence. He smiled and greeted Courtney cheerfully. They exchanged pleasantries. Courtney introduced Angie to her former co-worker.

"We've been wondering about the murder. No one's been caught," Angie told Mr. Adams.

"We've been trying to piece together who might have had motive." Courtney leaned against the registration counter.

Adams snorted. "Half the town of Sweet Cove, that's who had motive. And that's probably a gross under-estimation."

Angie agreed. "He wasn't popular, that's for sure."

"Did you ever notice Finch fighting or arguing with anyone? Ever hear any threats?" Courtney asked Mr. Adams.

Adams grunted. "Naw. Just the usual barking from Finch. Nothing out of the ordinary. Don't know why I took that job. People warned me." He waved his hand in the air indicating the lobby. "Working here is like a breath of fresh air. We shouldn't have to put up with poor treatment from an employer for even one day."

"Did you notice anything that last evening you worked

there?" Angie questioned. "Did Finch leave at his regular time?"

Adams nodded, and then said, "Wait. No, he didn't. I remember because it was always such a relief when he left for the day. He was lurking around that night. It wasn't that busy, just a few customers. In fact, he told me I could go home early, he'd close up."

"*He* waited on the customers?" Courtney's eyes widened. "*He* closed up that night?"

"I know, huh. I thought it was strange, too." Adams adjusted his glasses.

"Who was in the shop when he told you to leave?" Angie wondered if that might have triggered Finch's desire to be alone in the shop with someone.

Adams stroked his chin. "Nobody from town. A few tourists. An older couple. Let me think … there was a family with a couple of kids. I remember because Finch didn't like kids."

"Why would Finch offer to wait on them?" Courtney's forehead was scrunched.

Adams' gray caterpillar eyebrows pinched close together. "Someone else came in right before Finch told me to leave for the night. It was the new manager from the resort."

"Really?' Angie asked. "The manager?"

"Did he and Finch speak to each other before you were told to go home?" Courtney lowered her voice.

"I can't remember. I was busy waiting on the family and the older couple."

"Did anything else seem off that night?" Courtney asked.

Adams shrugged a shoulder. "Not that I recall. Things

seemed normal, except for being told to finish my shift early and go home."

After a few moments, Courtney thanked Mr. Adams and wished him well in his new job. The girls stepped out into the sunlight.

"Remember Josh told me the manager of the resort has been acting oddly. He disappeared for a whole day without notice," Angie said. "It's unusual that Finch told Mr. Adams to go home right after the resort manager came into the store."

"I wonder if there's a link." Courtney fished in her pocket for an elastic band to use to tie her hair into a ponytail. "I wonder if Finch was attacked in the shop that night. I assumed he was killed early the next morning, just before we got there, but that must be wrong."

"We should ask Chief Martin about that. We should make sure he knows that Mr. Adams went home early that night." Angie eyed the ice cream stand. She turned to Courtney and they both said at the same time, "Want some ice cream?" They shared a laugh as they went to stand in line.

"I should ask Josh if he knows if the manager was gone from the resort the night of the murder. If the manager left for a while, then maybe Josh knows when he returned to the resort," Angie said.

"It would be interesting if we could put together a time line," Courtney noted. "Find out if the manager was gone until after Finch usually closed the shop."

"Let's talk to Josh." Angie ordered their ice creams at the take-out window.

Courtney made a mock sweet face. "I bet you won't mind that one bit."

14

When Angie and Courtney arrived home from interviewing Mr. Adams, Ellie and Attorney Ford were sitting together at the dining room table. Seeing the attorney, a chill gripped Angie's stomach.

Ford handed a folder to Ellie and she stood up. She saw her sisters and said, "Oh, you're back. I just finished going over the papers with Mr. Ford. We can look them over together later tonight."

Angie, Courtney, and Ford nodded at each other. Angie glanced up at the China cabinet where Euclid and Circe were perched. She wondered what the cats thought of Ford.

Ellie called to Mr. Finch who was in the living room talking with the Foleys about art. "Mr. Finch, Attorney Ford is ready for you."

Mr. Finch was retaining Attorney Ford to help him with his brother's estate. Finch rose from the sofa, took hold of his cane, and crossed the foyer. He tipped an imaginary hat to Angie and Courtney as he passed. They smiled at him.

Angie and Courtney headed for Jenna's shop. They wanted to tell her what they'd heard from Mr. Adams and get her opinion on things. Jenna sat at her desk by the window and looked up when they came in.

"Did you have a visitor this morning? Did someone drop by to have coffee with you?' Courtney sank onto the sofa and eyed her sister.

Jenna shifted her eyes back to the piece of jewelry she was working on and asked coyly, "Who do you mean?"

Angie took a seat next to Jenna's desk to get a look at the latest necklace design. "Oooh, it's pretty. Such beautiful stones." She glanced at her twin sister. "We saw Tom's truck turning in here when we were walking down to the beach."

"He stopped by to say hello." Jenna kept her focus on the intricate work she was completing, but Angie could see a tinge of pink on her cheeks.

"If you'd stop blushing every time we mention Tom, we'd stop teasing you about him." Courtney pulled her legs up on the sofa and stretched out. "It's just too much fun."

Angie made eye contact with Jenna. "She's right, you know."

Jenna groaned. "It's like living with two middle school kids."

Angie chuckled.

In order to change the subject, Jenna asked, "What happened with Mr. Adams?"

Courtney reported what Adams had said about dead Finch sending him home early the night of the murder and who was in the shop at the time.

Jenna turned in her seat to better face her sisters. "So, Finch was probably killed that night, not the next morning. It must have happened before he closed up because the door to the candy store was open when you arrived in the morning, but the front lights weren't on. He probably turned off the lights just as he was leaving and then somebody attacked him."

Angie nodded. "Seems likely. I wonder if Chief Martin would confirm the time of death to us."

"Maybe Finch was expecting someone that night and that's why he sent Mr. Adams home early." Jenna ran her finger tip over one of the gemstones on her desk. "Or maybe someone came in to the shop that Finch wasn't expecting and he sent Adams home because of that."

"I think it's because someone came in that he wasn't expecting," Courtney said. "Otherwise, why wouldn't he just tell Mr. Adams ahead of time that he could leave early?"

"Good point." Angie held the new necklace up to her throat and leaned down to see her reflection in the small mirror Jenna kept on her desk.

Ellie peeked into the room. "Angie, Attorney Ford asked if he could speak to you for a minute."

Angie whirled towards her sister still holding the jewelry up to her neck. A nervous chill always skittered over her skin whenever she had to face Ford. "Why does he want to talk to me?"

"He didn't say." Ellie's face disappeared from the doorway.

Angie returned the gemstone piece to Jenna's desk.

"You want me to come with you?" Jenna asked.

Angie let out a sigh. "He'll just insist it's a private conversation, which is nonsense, because I will tell you anyway." She trudged to the door and walked down the hallway.

Ford was standing in the foyer waiting for her. "Ah, Ms. Roseland." He looked into the living room, but saw the Foleys still sitting in there, so he gestured to the dining room.

Euclid was still on top of the cabinet. He sat up when Angie and Ford entered the dining area.

Euclid's presence made Angie feel better. "You wanted to talk to me, Mr. Ford?"

"The court proceedings on Professor Linden's will are moving forward. The estate may well be settled sooner than we thought."

Angie's heart skipped a beat with excitement.

Ford said, "Perhaps, things will be settled by the beginning of July."

"That's wonderful news." Angie actually smiled at Ford.

"I'm glad for you." Ford clasped his hands in front of him.

Angie hesitated, but emboldened by Ford's almost genial manner, she asked, "I was wondering something." She paused. "Does client confidentiality continue after the client is dead?"

Ford stood straighter. "Client confidentiality remains intact even when the client is deceased."

"I see." Angie's disappointment was evident on her face.

"What is your question in reference to, Ms. Roseland?"

Angie pushed a strand of her honey hair behind her ear. "It was in reference to what Professor Linden asked you concerning her father shortly before she died." Angie glanced up at Euclid to gauge his reaction to the conversation. The orange cat sat quietly looking down at them. Angie went on, "And in reference to why you were in this house on the evening after Professor Linden was killed."

Ford released an almost imperceptible sigh. "I thought the discussion we had about that was sufficient."

"I don't think it was." Angie's expression hardened.

Ford shook his head. "I have nothing else to add to it." He moved to the dining table and picked up his briefcase. "Is that all, Ms. Roseland?"

Angie said nothing.

"I'll be on my way, then." Ford took three steps towards the front door and stopped. He turned back to Angie and looked at her for several seconds. "I'm on your side, Ms. Roseland."

When Angie made eye contact with Ford, she was surprised to sense sincerity coming from the man.

Ford started across the foyer to the door. He halted, turned back again, and took several brisk steps until he stood right in front of Angie. He lowered his voice to almost a whisper. "You have questions about Professor Linden's father."

Angie nodded.

Ford's eyes were dark and serious. "Maybe you should do some research on him." He held Angie's eyes. "Have a nice day, Ms. Roseland."

15

"The paperwork looks fine to me. And I like the official name." Angie smiled and handed the folder to Jenna who opened it and started to read the forms. "The Sweet Dreams Bed and Breakfast Inn."

Courtney and Ellie had already read the paperwork and given their opinions. They carried two kinds of burritos, rice, and salad into the family room and placed the dishes on the coffee table.

Jenna joined them on the sofas. "It all looks in order to me, too." She handed the folder to Ellie who placed it on the side table.

"Good. That's taken care of, then. I'll sign the papers and return them to Attorney Ford." Ellie handed a plate to Jenna.

They dug into the food and filled their plates. While they munched, Angie told them about her conversation with Ford.

"What could he mean about doing research on the professor's father?" Jenna asked.

"I have no idea," Angie said. "But it was clear he was telling me to find out about the man."

Courtney lifted a forkful of beef burrito to her mouth. "Delicious, Angie." She chewed and swallowed. "Ford told you he was on your side."

"Yes."

Ellie passed the salsa to Angie. "Interesting. Maybe he does have our best interests in mind."

"I'm still going to be wary of him." Courtney wiped her chin. "Angie says I think everyone has to prove their innocence."

Jenna chuckled. "Then you're in the wrong country. Here we believe people are innocent until proven guilty."

"That's fine for the courts, but we need to protect ourselves. It doesn't hurt to be careful," Courtney said.

Angie finished the last bite of her veggie burrito. "Do you think Ford was in the house the night the professor died because he really was looking for the most recent will?"

"Maybe he *is* trying to help you." Courtney gave small pieces of beef from her burrito to Euclid and Circe. "Let's look up Professor Linden's father and see what we can discover about him."

"I'm surprised Circe is in here with us." Ellie patted the black cat. "She spends a lot of time skulking around in my office. Sometimes, she just stares at the wall."

"She stares at the wall?" Angie gave the cat a quizzical look.

"I'm always worried she's staring at a mouse or something." Ellie shuddered.

"Which wall?" Jenna asked. "Show us."

The four of them wandered down the hall to the office. "That wall." Ellie pointed to the far side of the room.

The girls went in. Courtney tapped lightly against the wall while Angie put her ear against it. Circe jumped up on the desk and meowed.

"Huh," Angie said. "Maybe we have mice in there. We should watch for any signs of them in the kitchen."

Circe let out another meow.

Courtney scratched the cat's ears. "We'll figure out if we have mice in there, little one. Don't worry."

They filed back into the family room to sit and finish their meals.

"We should talk about the murder. I feel like our ideas are going in circles." Angie put her empty plate on the table.

"Let's make a list of suspects." Courtney got up and took a pen and some paper from the desk near the window. She returned to her seat. "There's Mr. Finch."

"It's not Mr. Finch. He didn't kill his brother." Jenna shook her head.

"How do you know for sure?" Ellie asked.

Jenna said, "Well, for one thing, the cats like him."

"True." Courtney drew a pen line through Finch's name. "That's good enough for me. I crossed him off the list."

"You're going to cross him off the list on the basis of two cats' reactions to him?" Ellie asked.

Her three sisters stared at her.

"Oh, okay." Ellie gave in with a groan.

"Do we have any suspects?" Courtney looked around at her sisters. "No one?"

Angie said, "Well, what about the manager of the resort?

He was seen in the candy store the evening Finch was murdered. Josh told me his name is Andrew Flynn. Mr. Adams said that Flynn was in the candy store when Finch told him he didn't need to finish his shift and that he could go home for the night."

"And you said that Josh told you that Flynn has been a problem. Disappearing when he's supposed to be working," Jenna said.

"I should talk to Josh. See if he knows if Flynn was supposed to be working the night of the murder." Angie pulled out her phone and texted Josh to ask about Andrew Flynn.

"Any other suspects?" Courtney asked.

Jenna said, "What about Lindsay, the assistant manager from the Pirate's Den. She told Angie that dead Finch was really mean to her when she worked for him a couple of years ago. He made nasty comments about her weight and accused her of stealing from the store. Maybe she took revenge on him."

Angie pondered the possibility. "Good idea. I'd put her on the suspect list."

Courtney wrote the name on the list and then tapped the pen on the arm of the sofa. "The problem is that no one knew Finch. He was never seen around town, didn't take part in anything in town. He had no friends, wasn't married. He worked and went home. That was it."

Ellie said, "He collected art."

"Let's look him up on the internet. See if he belonged to any clubs or organizations." Jenna pulled out her phone and tapped at it.

"I doubt that dead Finch belonged to anything. He

wasn't sociable at all." Ellie started to clear away the dinner plates from the coffee table.

"We should talk to the Walsh sisters," Courtney said.

"Why them?" Ellie asked.

"They worked part time at the candy store. They always worked the same shifts together. They split the paycheck between them. I guess when you're in your late eighties you get to do what you want."

Angie laughed. "Dead Finch got two employees for the price of one."

Courtney nodded. "He needed employees and there aren't many people around here who were willing to work for him, so he took what he could get."

"Is that why he hired you?" Jenna teased.

Courtney scowled at her sister.

"I have to tease you when I get the chance. I need to get back at you for all the razzing you dish out over Tom." Jenna tapped at her phone again. "Nothing comes up on the internet about dead Finch except information on the candy shop and his prizes and awards."

"That figures. The man is a mystery." Angie turned to Courtney. "Let's go see the Walsh sisters tomorrow."

"If nothing else," Courtney said, "we'll get all the town gossip. The Walsh's know everything that's going on in Sweet Cove."

Angie's phone buzzed with an incoming text. "It's from Josh." She read the message. "Josh says that Andrew Flynn requested the evening off the night that Finch was killed."

"Well, well," Ellie said. Her eyes narrowed.

Courtney picked up the pen and placed a star next to

Andrew Flynn's name on her list of suspects. "Someone just went to the top of the list."

16

When Angie and Courtney knocked on the Walsh sisters' door, no one answered. As they turned away and started down the walkway, they heard yelling in the backyard of the house. They hurried to see if someone needed help. When they reached the rear of the home, Mildred Walsh stood beside a covered back porch swatting at hornets buzzing about her. Her sister Agnes had a broom in her hands and looked to have just knocked a hornet's nest from the roof of the porch. Angie and Courtney rushed to Mildred's aid, but by then the aggressive insects had fled.

"Did they bite you?' Courtney asked.

"A few bites, but I'm not allergic. Awful little creatures." Mildred's voice was hoarse and raspy from years of smoking. She rubbed at the red welts rising on the skin of her arm. She glanced at her sister who was hurrying over to her. "Next time, I'll use the broom on them. Little devils."

Agnes's worried expression changed to one of relief. "Goodness. I guess that wasn't the best way to get rid of hornets." Agnes was dressed in jeans and a hooded sweatshirt. From behind, she could pass for a teenager. She blinked at Angie and Courtney. "What brings you girls to the rescue?"

"We knocked at the front door and heard yelling back here," Courtney said.

Angie asked, "We wanted to chat with you both. Do you want to go inside, Mildred, and put something on those bites?"

"Bah. No need. The welts will go down eventually. Come sit on the porch." She led the way to the wicker seats and table on the covered back porch. They sat down.

"Can we get you something to drink?" Agnes asked the girls.

"Nothing, thanks." Angie shook her head. "We don't want to take too much of your time."

"What's on your minds?" Mildred rubbed at her arm.

"We've been talking about Mr. Finch's murder," Courtney told them. "We've been thinking about who might have killed him. We wondered if either of you had seen something suspicious or heard an argument or anything like that."

"Finch." Mildred practically spit the word out of her mouth. "That nasty old goat. Got what was coming to him, I say."

"Mildred." Agnes chastised her sister. "That isn't charitable."

"Did Finch deserve better then he got?" Mildred asked. Agnes didn't answer.

Courtney asked, "How did Finch treat you?"

"Like we were old hags who could barely do anything right." Mildred scowled.

"Why did you keep working there?" Angie asked.

Agnes said, "We like to keep active, get out and meet people. We could work together at the candy store, not many places allow that. Together we felt like we could deal with Mr. Finch. Neither of us would put up with him if we were working there alone."

Mildred added, "Finch basically left us alone after we were trained. He'd hide in the back room making the products. We liked interacting with the customers."

"Finch thought we were stupid old ladies," Agnes confided. "We played the part. We let him think that's what we were." She chuckled.

"You talk to a lot of people in town," Angie said. "Is there any gossip about who might have killed Finch?"

"Oh, I don't know." Agnes fiddled with the ring on her finger. "People talk, sure, but no one knows anything."

"Oh, just tell them, Agnes," Mildred said. "They're nice girls."

Angie and Courtney exchanged a quick glance. Neither said anything waiting to see if Agnes would speak.

"Well." Agnes lowered her voice. "Our friend works at the dry cleaner up the road."

"Yes?" Angie wished she would just say what she knew.

"He said someone dropped off a suit to be cleaned." Agnes paused.

Mildred spoke up, "Oh for heaven's sake, Agnes, just tell them." She looked across the table at the girls. "There was blood on the suit."

Agnes leaned forward. "A lot of blood."

"Really?' Courtney wanted more information. "Did the man say how the blood got on the suit?

"He said that there was an accident." Agnes clucked her tongue to the roof of her mouth.

Angie and Courtney weren't sure what that meant. "What?"

Mildred narrowed her eyes. "Our friend didn't believe the man's explanation. Our friend said that a man like that, who dressed like that, would never get close to any blood."

"When did this happen?" Courtney asked.

"Right after Finch got killed." Mildred looked smug.

Angie asked, "Did your friend tell the police?"

"Nah," Mildred waved her hand dismissively. "Cleaners see all kinds of weird stuff. Can't run to the police over every little thing."

"Did your friend know the man who came in with the suit?" Courtney questioned.

"He'd never seen him before," Agnes said.

"What about his name? Did he have to leave his name?"

"No. People just give their phone number when they drop things off." Mildred checked the welts on her arm. "Look, the bumps are going down already."

"Would your friend still have the man's number? Would he tell us what it is?" Angie asked.

Agnes and Mildred exchanged looks.

"We could ask him," Agnes offered.

"Would you mind?" Angie asked. "It could prove very helpful."

"We'll let you know. Leave us your number and we'll call you if we find out." Mildred went inside the house and returned with a piece of paper and a pen.

Angie wrote her name and number on the paper and handed it back. "Thanks so much."

* * *

Angie and Courtney hurried up the sidewalk.

"Wow, this could be a break in the case." Courtney rubbed her hands together. "Should we tell Chief Martin?"

Angie said, "Maybe we should wait and see if the dry cleaner can report the man's number. It's probably true that cleaners see strange things. I guess they can't jump to conclusions and report everything. We can always tell the chief later."

"What should we do next?" Courtney asked. "We've talked to all the candy shop employees."

"I guess now we wait to see if the cleaner gives the Walsh sisters the phone number of the guy with the bloody suit. Why don't we head home and see if Ellie needs any help with the B and B tasks." An idea flickered in Angie's mind. "Then what about a trip to the town hall or library to start looking for information about Professor Linden's father?"

"Sounds good to me, but what do you want to know about him?"

"I wonder what Professor Linden asked Attorney Ford about her father. Why would she ask Ford? What could Ford possibly know about her father? What was she looking for?" Angie's forehead was creased as she pondered the questions. "And why would Attorney Ford tell me to look up Professor Linden's father?"

"Another mystery." Courtney shook her head. "Do you

ever wonder why Professor Linden left you the Victorian?"

"Every single day," Angie replied. "I think about it all the time."

Courtney said, "I know you were nice to the Professor, but is that enough reason for her to leave you the house and the money? There seems like there should be more to it."

Angie looked at her sister. "Exactly."

"Do you think Professor Linden's father might hold a clue to it?"

Angie sighed. "We won't know until we look."

Courtney's eyes widened. "Do you think Attorney Ford knows the reason why Professor Linden left you her property?"

"That thought has occurred to me." A breeze blew a strand of Angie's hair into her eyes and she pushed it back behind her ear. "But I don't think there's any chance that Ford is going to give me that information."

"We'll just have to discover the answer on our own." Courtney put her hand on her sister's shoulder and gave it a squeeze.

Angie's phone buzzed and when she answered the call she was surprised to hear Mildred Walsh's voice. She listened for several seconds then asked Courtney for a pen and a piece of paper. Courtney rummaged through her small handbag and pulled out a pencil and an old receipt. Angie wrote something down, thanked Mildred and ended the call.

She smiled at Courtney. "This is the phone number from the dry cleaners. He said it's the number the man with the bloody suit gave him."

"Those Walsh sisters don't waste any time." Courtney

read the numbers on the back of the receipt. "Now we just need to find out who it belongs to."

The girls turned onto the walkway leading to the Victorian's front porch.

"Wait until Jenna and Ellie hear this," Courtney said.

The girls bounded up the steps and went inside the house.

17

The sisters gathered in Jenna's jewelry room and while Angie told Ellie and Jenna what they'd learned from the Walsh sisters, Courtney used her phone to access the internet and look up the number the dry cleaner had produced.

"How are you finding who the number belongs to?" Ellie asked.

"I'm using a reverse phone number site." Courtney stared at the screen on her phone and tapped at it. "Sometimes it works and sometimes it doesn't."

Angie paced around the room. "Are you finding anything?"

"Nothing on that last site." She continued tapping. "Wait. Here it is." Her voice quivered with excitement. She raised her eyes to her three sisters.

"What?" Jenna asked. "What did you find?"

"It belongs to Andrew Flynn."

"The resort manager?" Ellie asked.

"No way." Angie rushed across the room to see the information on Courtney's phone.

"That's an interesting development." Jenna stood up and joined the circle of sisters passing the phone back and forth. Once she saw Flynn's name and number on the small screen, she went back to her desk and opened her laptop. "Let's look him up. See what's out there on him." Her sisters crowded around her laptop.

"Wow," Ellie said. "He's worked all over the world."

"It looks like he has a strong reputation." Jenna scrolled through the information. "There are lots of admiring comments about his service."

Angie said, "Josh told me that Flynn comes with strong recommendations. Josh thought they hit the jackpot when he accepted their offer to work at the resort."

"Why would he choose to work in a little town like Sweet Cove?" Courtney asked. "After living in London, Paris, Geneva, why would he be drawn to the resort? It seems like a step down from what he's done. It seems like quite a few steps down."

Ellie offered, "Maybe he's tired of a high-powered environment?"

"It seems like professional suicide." Jenna said, "Flynn is only in middle-age. I could see making a change to something simpler later in life, but now? I don't buy it."

"Should we talk to Chief Martin?" Courtney asked.

"Maybe we'd better." Angie frowned at the thought that Flynn moved to Sweet Cove with malicious intent. "I think

I'll talk it over with Josh. We're going on a bike ride in a couple of days."

"Oh, really?" Jenna prepared to go into full teasing mode, but Mr. Finch's voice called from the hallway.

Ellie started out of the room to go and see what Finch wanted. Angie was right on her heels in order to escape from Jenna.

Jenna said, "You can stay here, Angie. Ellie can take care of Mr. Finch."

Angie pretended she didn't hear Jenna's comment and hurried down the hallway to the foyer.

Mr. Finch, dressed in his usual suit jacket and tie, stood next to Betty Hayes, the town Realtor. "Hello." He beamed a smile at Angie and Ellie.

Betty greeted the sisters. Her voice had a girlish tone and she seemed to be batting her eyes at Mr. Finch. Angie knew that Betty would do just about anything to get a listing, but she almost seemed to be flirting with Mr. Finch. For a few seconds, Angie worried that Betty had eaten something she'd baked recently and somehow it had put a love spell on her.

"You know the lovely, Ms. Hayes?" Finch asked the girls as he smiled at Betty.

Ellie and Angie exchanged surprised glances. They both nodded.

"I didn't realize you knew each other." Angie blinked.

"I've only recently had the good fortune to make Ms. Hayes' acquaintance."

"Victor ... um ... Mr. Finch contacted me to talk about real estate for sale in the area." She gave him a coy smile.

"We met for lunch and discovered that we share many of the same interests." A pink color flushed Betty's cheeks.

Angie and Ellie couldn't believe what they were witnessing.

"Are you planning to stay in Sweet Cove, Mr. Finch?" Ellie asked.

"I would love to. I wondered if you had any availability here at the B and B for the next several weeks. I'm planning to house-hunt and move into my own place as soon as I can."

"It will be very nice to have you as part of the Sweet Cove community," Angie told him.

"What about your brother's house? You aren't interested in moving in there?" Ellie asked.

Finch's face lost its joy. "Never. I would never live in Thaddeus' house. Call it superstitious, but I don't want to make my home in a place with such bad karma."

"Mr. Finch wants to make a home in a house of his choosing. And, rightly so." Betty beamed at him.

Angie hoped that Betty's feelings were genuine and that she wasn't manipulating Mr. Finch.

"We can certainly accommodate you here at the B and B. In fact, I'll juggle some reservations so that you can stay in your room for as long as you need to. We're happy to have you here. I'll go see to those changes right away." Ellie went to her office to make the reservation adjustments.

Angie gestured to the dining room. "Ellie has the afternoon refreshments out. Help yourself."

Mr. Finch placed his hand on Betty's elbow and gently directed her to the buffet table. Angie was struck by how

happy they seemed together. She couldn't believe her eyes.
What next?

* * *

While watching Betty and Finch, Angie's phone buzzed.
It was a text from Josh asking if she was free and would she
like to go for a bike ride. Angie's heart beat speeded up. Her
fingers flew over the letters on the phone replying in the af-
firmative.

Angie met Josh in the driveway of the Victorian. When
he pulled up, he stopped, straddled his bike and took his
helmet off. His sandy blonde hair was covered with a light
sheen of sweat. Angie melted from his smile.

"I'm so glad you could bike today. Davis is commanding
my attendance at some meetings in New Hampshire, so I'm
going to be gone for a week." Josh's brother Davis was trying to close several business development deals while Josh
was dealing with the management issues at the Sweet Cove
resort.

"How are the manager problems?" Angie attached her
water bottle to her bike and slipped her cell phone into the
small saddlebag.

"It's ongoing, I'm afraid." Josh scowled. "I'm not sure
what we're going to do. That's something Davis and I will
talk about once I get to New Hampshire."

"I want to talk to you about your manager, but let's
head off. What I want to talk to you about can wait." Angie
hopped onto her bicycle. Josh put his helmet on, and the two

pedaled away up Beach Street heading to the main street that would take them out of town and northward up the coast.

The afternoon sun was strong, but the speed of the bikes provided a cool breeze that kept Angie and Josh's body temperatures comfortable. The movement and rhythm warmed Angie's muscles and the exercise cleared her head and refreshed her. After eight miles, they followed a country road heading inland. They past green, rolling hills and sections of wooded areas where the trees made a canopy over the road. The temperature dropped noticeably in the shade.

Josh suggested they take a break up ahead and he and Angie pulled off the road into a park which was part of the Yorktown Hospital. They pedaled the bikes to a bench placed under a tree on a grassy area next to the hospital parking lot.

"It feels great to be out and moving." Angie took a swallow from her water container. She pulled a couple of granola bars from her saddlebag and handed one to Josh.

"Homemade?" Josh removed the bar from its wrapping.

Angie nodded.

Josh took a bite. "It's delicious." He smiled at her as he chewed. "Like all the things you make."

Angie felt her cheeks warm. Sitting close to Josh on the bench, she smelled his slightly spicy smell and it almost made her swoon.

"You wanted to talk to me about the resort manager?" Josh took another bite of his bar.

Angie told Josh her concerns about Andrew Flynn and how the dry cleaner claimed there was blood on the suit that Flynn dropped off to be cleaned. "He is probably innocent, but I thought I'd let you know what we found out."

"It's definitely disconcerting. He has seemed very distracted and he continues to leave the resort at odd times when he's supposed to be working." Josh shook his head. "I dislike confrontation. I've asked him if anything was wrong, but he just brushes my questions aside or makes some lame excuse. I don't understand him. We were thrilled about hiring Flynn. Now it's become a real thorn in my side."

Angie took another drink of water. "I'm sorry something you were happy about has turned sour."

Josh adjusted his position on the bench so that he could see Angie's face better. "You're very kind, you know."

Angie's heart flipped. Josh's gaze warmed her whole body. She felt herself melting into the bench and wondered how she would propel herself off of it since all of her muscles were now goo.

Movement in the parking lot near them caught Angie's attention. She squinted and leaned forward. A man pushed an older woman in a wheelchair and stopped next to a black SUV. He opened the door of the passenger side and moved the wheelchair closer.

"Josh. Look there." Angie pointed at the man in the lot.

"What? Where?" Josh shifted his eyes from Angie to where she was pointing.

"Is that your resort manager?" Angie took a good look.

Josh squinted from the sun's glare. "It is. It's Andrew."

They watched him place his hand under the woman's arm and help her stand so that she could shift onto the seat of the vehicle. The woman had short gray hair. Her frame was frail and small. Her hands and arms were bandaged. She moved like a rag doll. Flynn seated the woman and buckled her seatbelt.

Josh stood up and strode towards the car. "Andrew!"

Angie followed Josh through the parking lot.

Flynn seemed startled to hear his name called and when he spotted Josh coming towards him, his face remained blank for a few seconds until he recognized his employer.

"Josh." Flynn took two steps away from the SUV.

"How unexpected to see you here." Josh introduced Angie. "Is everything okay?"

Flynn seemed to wrestle with his answer, but then said, "My mother." He gestured to the woman in his car. "She's been unwell for quite some time. My sister cares for her. It's become much too difficult." He hesitated. "This is the reason I took the job at the resort, to be closer to my mother and to help my sister." He quickly added, "Of course, I love the resort and Sweet Cove…."

Josh finished Flynn's sentence. "But it's not what you're used to. I understand." Josh glanced at the woman in the car. She appeared disengaged from her surroundings. "Why didn't you tell me what you've been dealing with?"

Flynn shrugged. "I didn't think it professional to burden you with my personal issues. I've been evasive about it. I apologize. I thought I could handle it without it interfering with the work."

"There's no need to apologize." Josh put his hand on Flynn's shoulder. "Take the time you need to care for your family. That's most important. We'll adjust at the resort to accommodate what you need. No worries."

A burden seemed to lift from Flynn. Tension seemed to recede from his facial muscles. "I appreciate it."

Angie glanced at the woman's bandages. "Did she burn herself?"

Flynn looked from his mother to Angie. "No. She's suffering from dementia. Sometimes she sees things that aren't there. She imagined an intruder. She had a knife and ended up cutting her hands and arms, pretty badly. I tried to stop her. It took quite an effort to subdue her."

"I'm very sorry," Angie told him. *That's why he had blood on his suit.*

"We're moving her to an assisted living facility. Right now, in fact. It's for her safety."

Josh shook Flynn's hand. "Good luck. Take a few days if you need to."

Angie and Josh returned to their bikes.

Angie picked up her helmet. "I'm sorry for Flynn's troubles. Now we know how he got the blood on his suit."

Josh lifted his bike from the ground. "I'm glad we ran into him. It clears everything up. It's a relief."

Angie got on her bicycle. "And it clears him as a suspect, too."

Josh put on his helmet. "It's a strange coincidence … us running into him here like that."

Angie nodded. She wondered if somehow something led them here. *I was in the lead during our bike ride. Did I know Flynn would be here?* The idea made her uncomfortable. She rubbed her temple.

They pedaled away and headed back towards Sweet Cove. For the rest of the outing, questions swirled in Angie's mind. *So Flynn didn't murder Finch. Then who is the killer?*

At the end of their ride, Angie and Josh turned their bikes into the Victorian's driveway.

"That was great." Josh removed his helmet. "I'm so glad we were able to ride together today."

"Would you like to come inside for a cold drink?" Angie

held her helmet and ran her hand through her hair.

"I'll have to take a rain check. I need to get back to the resort. There's an anniversary party booked there tonight that I have to check on. I'll need to fill in for Andrew."

Angie's heart sank when Josh told her that he wouldn't be able to come inside for a drink. "I'm glad we ran into Andrew today and got all that sorted out."

"I'm thankful that I know the reason that Andrew has been so distracted. I'll fill in for him whenever he needs to be with his mother."

Angie hoped that would mean Josh would be around Sweet Cove for a while longer.

"I had a great day with you." Josh held Angie's eyes.

Warmth flooded Angie's body and her muscles tingled. "Me, too." She didn't want their time together to end.

Josh placed his hand on Angie's arm. He leaned down and moved his face close, and just as his lips brushed hers, the Victorian's front door opened and voices could be heard. Josh and Angie pulled apart.

Tom and Jenna stepped onto the porch and spotted Angie and Josh next to their bikes at the end of the driveway. They waved. Angie was glad they weren't close enough to notice her rosy cheeks.

"Um." Josh smiled at Angie. "I'll see you soon."

She nodded. "Thanks for a nice day."

Josh turned his bike and headed up Beach Street. Angie started to walk her bike down the driveway to store it in the carriage house, when she noticed Tom standing on the porch facing her. He held his fingers in the shape of a heart next to his chest. He puckered his lips and made a smooching sound.

Angie rolled her eyes at him, but couldn't keep her mouth from forming a big smile as she continued down the driveway with her bike.

18

Angie put her bicycle in the carriage house and went into the Victorian through the back door. She could hear voices in the kitchen, so she headed that way and was surprised to see Courtney and Mr. Finch working at the counter both wearing pink aprons. Euclid and Circe sat on top of the refrigerator watching the proceedings. "It smells delicious in here."

Courtney smiled at Angie. "Mr. Finch is teaching me how to make candy." Her sleeves were pushed up and she was rolling some chocolate substance between her palms. "Come see."

Mr. Finch winked at Angie. "It's a secret family recipe."

Courtney chuckled. "So don't try to figure out the ingredients."

Small balls of chocolates were lined up on a sheet of wax paper.

"Chocolate truffles." Mr. Finch indicated the rows of little balls. "Try one."

Angie lifted one to her mouth and ate. "Wow. Excellent. You two make a good team."

"Maybe I'll become a candymaker." Courtney dusted the balls with finely ground chocolate.

"I hope you do. It will benefit me." Angie smiled and licked her finger. She proceeded to tell Courtney and Finch about the resort manager and how he was no longer a suspect.

"I was sure it was him." Courtney carried the mixing bowl to the sink. "It's back to square one now."

"You know," Finch started, but then hesitated.

"What? Do you have an idea?" Angie waited for Finch to go on.

"I don't know." He glanced up at the cats and then made eye contact with Angie. "The cats don't seem to like Mr. or Mrs. Foley."

Euclid sat up and let out a low hiss.

"Euclid confirms your idea, Mr. Finch. Why don't you like them, Euclid? I wish you could talk." Angie had a pensive expression on her face. She looked at Courtney and Finch. "Do either of you get a feeling or a sense that something is wrong with the couple?"

Finch looked wide-eyed at Courtney. "You have a gift, too? You sense things?"

"Sometimes. It's still developing."

Finch smiled with delight. "How wonderful."

Courtney considered Angie's question. "Thinking about it, maybe I do get a sense of something being off. I thought it was just because I didn't like them much."

"Would you two use your perception the next time you're with the Foleys? See if you pick up on anything." Angie made eye contact with the cats. "Cats, see what you can find out."

Courtney shook hands with Mr. Finch and gave the thumbs up gesture to Euclid and Circe. "Don't worry, Angie. We're on the case."

* * *

Angie walked into Jenna's jewelry shop to tell her that the resort manager was innocent. Jenna was busy behind one of the display cases showing a pair of earrings to Lindsay, the assistant manager from the Pirate's Den restaurant. Two other women were browsing the cases.

Angie greeted Lindsay and asked the two women if she could show them something. They pointed to a necklace and matching earrings made of silver and sea glass pieces. Angie placed a slate gray velvet mat on top of the glass case and laid the jewelry on it. The women took turns lifting the necklace to their necks and peering in the mirror. The jewelry was going to be a gift for their mother. After some deliberation, the women agreed that the pieces were perfect and Angie boxed and wrapped the items and rang up the sale. The women left the shop chattering happily.

"How are things?" Angie asked Lindsay.

"The restaurant is getting busy now that the tourist season is beginning. I'm working a lot." Lindsay chose a pair of earrings from the two she had been considering. "This is the first afternoon I've had off in a long while."

Jenna said, "Lindsay's thinking of renting the candy shop

space once the investigation into the murder is complete."

"Really?" Angie's eyebrows went up.

"I'd like to open a sandwich shop." Lindsay removed some bills from her wallet to pay Jenna. "I've set aside some money. If I'm going to work as hard as I've been doing, it might as well benefit me."

Angie nodded in agreement. "That's great. I hope it works out."

"You know how hard it is to find space that's available to rent. You tried to find reasonable space with a good location in town when you found out your bake shop lease wouldn't be renewed." Lindsay waited for Jenna to wrap her purchase.

"I couldn't find anything that would work for me." Angie leaned against the case.

"So when Finch died, I decided to jump on it." Lindsay took the bag from Jenna. "I talked to the Realtor and told her that I want the space as soon as it becomes available."

Angie asked, "You talked to Betty Hayes already?" She had a funny feeling that she couldn't place. Angie looked towards the hallway. She wished the cats would come in.

"I told Betty I wanted it. I think it's a perfect location and with the kitchen in the back, there'd be very little alterations needed." Lindsay headed for the shop door. "Thanks, Jenna. The earrings are beautiful." She left the jewelry store.

"Do you get a weird vibe from her?" Angie asked.

Jenna looked towards the door that Lindsay had just exited through. "I don't know. Like what? Like you don't trust her?"

"Sort of. She had a grudge against Finch. I wonder...."

Jenna said, "That's interesting that she wants Finch's storefront, isn't it?"

"She seems determined to grab the space when it becomes available." Angie leaned her elbow on the top of the jewelry case and held her chin in her hand. "She didn't say anything about what the rent will be. It didn't seem to concern her."

Jenna sat down at her desk. "Would hating Finch and wanting his store space be enough motive for her to...?"

Angie gave Jenna a pointed look. "People have done a lot of bad things with less motive than that."

Angie's phone buzzed. "It's Chief Martin." She answered and listened for several minutes. "We'll meet you there. See you soon." She turned to her sister. "Chief Martin wants me and Courtney to meet him at Finch's candy store. He said the investigation has stalled. He wants us to see if we can sense anything by being in the shop."

"Why don't you bring the cats with you?" From the look on her face, Jenna wasn't kidding about it.

Angie could feel a pricking at the back of her mind, and then the idea formed. "The night that Lisa Barrows tried to poison me just jumped into my head. I remember how I felt and how Euclid saved me by knocking the poisoned tea from my hand."

Jenna gave Angie a questioning look.

"Just before all that happened, I had been on Robin's Point. I felt the thrumming in my blood that I always feel when I'm there."

"Where are you going with this?" Jenna asked.

"Before we meet the chief, I think Courtney and I should go down to the point first, kind of get in touch with whatever happens to us when we're down there."

Jenna nodded. "It couldn't hurt."

The corners of Angie's mouth turned up in a slight smile. "And then, we'll come back and get the cats."

19

Angie and Courtney sat down on the grass where their grandmother's cottage once stood. The late afternoon sun warmed them as they watched people swimming and playing on the beach. To the right of the main beach, several surfers bobbed on the ocean swells waiting for a good wave to come up.

Courtney kicked her shoes off and wiggled her toes in the grass. "We need to get to the beach. We keep saying we'll go and then something comes up."

"The water looks really good. Maybe we can go this weekend." Angie looked sideways at her sister. "Do you feel anything?"

"Of course. I always do. Do you?"

Angie nodded. The familiar humming moved through her blood. Her muscles warmed and relaxed and Angie wasn't sure if it was the sun causing the pleasant sensation or if it was the thrumming that was doing it.

"It feels good." Courtney leaned back on the ground and closed her eyes.

Angie stretched her legs out in front of her. She'd always been so concerned and worried about what she felt when she was on the point that she didn't allow herself to really experience it. Sitting in the grass, she focused her attention to fully realize the vibration. She drifted off, not into slumber, but into a state of deep relaxation.

"We should probably go." Courtney nudged her sister and Angie's eyes flew open.

"How long have we been here?" Angie rubbed her eyes.

"Forty-five minutes."

Angie pushed herself up and stood. "I completely lost track of time."

"We better get going. We need to swing by the Victorian to pick up the cats and get to Finch's shop to meet the chief." Courtney pulled the elastic off her ponytail and shook out her hair.

The girls got into Angie's car and they headed back to the house to pick up Euclid and Circe.

Courtney's hair blew around her face from the breeze coming in the open car window. "Some people might think we're kind of strange to believe that the cats can be helpful finding clues to a murder."

Steering the car up Main Street, Angie gave Courtney a quick glance. "Not long ago, I was one of those people."

"You know what?" Courtney chuckled. "So was I."

* * *

Courtney opened the candy store door and pushed it with her shoulder. She carried Circe in her arms. Angie followed them in carrying Euclid. The orange cat looked slightly put out that he was being held like a baby. When Angie put him on the floor, he stretched and licked his fur into place.

Chief Martin came in from the back room and his eyes widened in surprise. "Oh, the cats. Well, very good."

Euclid and Circe moved silently about the room taking in the sights and smells.

The chief said, "I thought it could be helpful to have you come back in here and just sort of wander around. As I told Angie on the phone, the investigation is sort of dead in the water. We haven't given up by any means. Something new will come up, but, in the meantime, I figured it couldn't hurt to have you come back and look around."

"We're glad to try and help." Angie told the chief what she and her sisters had been thinking about who might be suspects. He nodded, but didn't say much. Angie knew he wasn't able to divulge anything from an ongoing case.

Courtney walked about the room. She ran her hand over the candy cases. "Someone needs to clean out the candy," she told the chief.

Angie walked into the back room to see what the cats were doing. Each one had gone in a different direction. Euclid sniffed around the walk-in refrigerator. Circe sat on Finch's desk and stared up at the book shelves above her head. Angie noticed the blood stain on the floor where Finch had fallen. She quickly shifted her gaze away from the spot. Euclid moved to gingerly sniff at the bloodstain. Chief

Martin entered the room. He pulled the chair away from the desk and settled onto the seat. His shoulders sagged.

The room still retained the scent of chocolate, sugar, and butter. The sinks, countertops, and all the equipment were spotless. Finch had cleaned and put everything away for the night before the killer intruded into the space. Angie made a circle around the back room and approached the chief in his chair. She shrugged and shook her head. The cats continued to meander about the room.

"I don't get a sense of anything at all. I'm sorry."

The chief hauled himself out the seat. "It was worth a try."

"Is Courtney still out front?" Angie walked over to the door. She stopped short. The chief came up behind her.

Courtney stood behind one of the candy cases. Her eyes stared across the room at nothing. Her face was pale.

"Courtney?" Angie took a step towards her sister, but the chief put his hand on Angie's shoulder to stop her.

After a few moments, Courtney shuddered and she sucked in a breath of air. She put her hand up to her forehead. Angie rushed to her side and placed her hand on Courtney's arm. "Are you okay?"

Courtney blinked several times before shaking off her stupor. "Angie." Her voice was just above a whisper.

"Did you sense something?"

"Finch was in the back room. There was talking ... then, shouting. The energy in the room was chaotic, dark. I saw a knife. And then Finch was on the floor."

The chief asked, "The voices you heard. Was it a man's voice? A woman's?"

Courtney's forehead creased. She turned to the chief. "Both."

"Was the man's voice Finch or someone else?"

"I'm not sure." She shook her head. "I don't know for certain."

"Could you see anything?" the chief asked.

"Just the glint of the knife, and only for a second."

A crash sounded in the back room and the three of them jumped. They rushed to see what had happened. A book had fallen or had been pushed by Circe off the top shelf. The chief pulled on surgical type gloves, leaned down, picked up the book, and turned it over in his hands.

"It's false."

"What?" Courtney asked.

"It's a fake book." He opened it. The inside had been hollowed out. The chief removed a leather notebook that was hidden inside and thumbed through it. "It's a list of transactions. It looks like a ledger of transactions. Seems to be for artwork purchases and sales. No names, just initials." The chief looked up. "Finch must have been dealing pieces of art."

"Illegally, it seems," Courtney said. "If it was legit, why would he hide the deals in a fake book?"

"Maybe this is how Finch became so wealthy." Angie peered over the chief's shoulder and stared at the notebook in his hands. "Was he dealing in stolen artwork?"

The chief let out a sigh. "Good question. This will take some research." He shifted his eyes to the black cat sitting on Finch's desk. "Thanks, Circe."

She trilled.

20

"My brother was dealing artwork?" Mr. Finch rocked gently in one of the front porch chairs with Circe asleep in his lap. "Thaddeus never ceases to amaze me. Were the pieces stolen?"

"Chief Martin doesn't know yet if the works were stolen or if your brother was handling the items as a broker bringing wealthy investors together to buy and sell." Angie placed a platter of ginger-molasses cookies on the small table near the rockers.

"It seems suspicious to me." Courtney sat on the floor of the porch with Euclid curled beside her. "If whatever he was doing was legal then why hide the paperwork? He had the information hidden in a fake book."

"I can't believe this. It's like a TV show or a movie." Jenna shook her head.

Tom had stopped by on his way to a new renovation project. He sipped an iced tea and reached for another of Angie's cookies. "What's going on around here? Is a small town a good cover for people who are up to no good? Is a small town like Sweet Cove a good hiding place because no one expects bad things to happen in a quaint, little town?"

"Could be." Jenna rocked beside Tom. "There has certainly been a lot going on here recently."

Ellie opened the front door and held it for Mr. and Mrs. Foley who carried suitcases and a carry-on bag. They bustled onto the porch. "We're off," Mrs. Foley smiled at everyone gathered outside.

Circe and Euclid woke and jumped onto the porch railing. They stared at the Foleys.

"I didn't realize you were leaving." Angie stepped forward to shake hands with the couple.

"We decided to cut our visit short by a few days." Mr. Foley placed his suitcase on the floor. "We've accomplished what we wanted from our visit."

Mrs. Foley said, "We saw so many of the sights. We had a lovely time. We're feeling well-rested and eager to get home for a week before we head off to Europe." She turned to Ellie. "I will be sure to leave you a five-star review for your lovely B and B."

The couple started down the steps with their things. Tom stood and went to help Mrs. Foley with her suitcase. "Let me get that," he offered.

"Oh, my, thank you. It was lovely meeting all of you." Mrs. Foley bustled to the car. She opened the passenger side door and placed her handbag on the seat.

Euclid leaped off the porch and ran to the vehicle. He jumped onto the roof of the car and sat there as Mr. Foley opened the trunk.

"Euclid," Jenna chastised the big orange cat.

"Come here, boy," Angie called to him.

Euclid sat like a statue. He would not budge.

Courtney started to laugh, but caught herself as a tingling sensation flowed through her body. She jerked her head towards Mr. Finch who had just pushed himself up from his rocker. He had a concerned expression on his face. Finch and Courtney made eye contact and the two of them hurried down the steps heading to the driveway. "I'll get Euclid," Courtney said.

The rushed way that Courtney and Finch walked to the driveway gave Angie a twinge of anxiety as she watched them from the porch.

Mr. Finch leaned on his cane and limped over to the car. When Courtney approached the side of the vehicle and reached up for the cat, Euclid slid down the rear window, jumped to the side, and hurtled into the trunk. Mrs. Foley cried out.

Mr. Finch sidled up to the open trunk. He pretended to be after Euclid, but his real intention was to get a look in the back hatch. Courtney joined him and the two of them rustled around the packed items of the trunk feigning an attempt to capture the cat.

"Oh, no, no. I'll take care if it." Mr. Foley used a mock cheerful tone as he tried to shoulder Finch and Courtney out of the way.

Euclid scratched at a plaid blanket that was draped over

an object that was pushed into the rear of the trunk. Mr. Foley's efforts to keep Courtney from reaching into the hatch became more aggressive and the young woman elbowed him in the side.

"Oh, sorry." She pretended she hadn't meant to jab him.

Once Euclid uncovered the object, he took a mighty leap from the vehicle over the heads of the people crowded at the rear of the car.

"What's this?" Mr. Finch reached forward to take hold of something that looked like a rolled up piece of carpet.

Foley tried to slam the trunk. Courtney blocked him.

Finch pulled the item forward.

Mr. Foley tried to grab the object out of Finch's hands. Finch leaned back and swatted Foley over the head with his cane. Mr. Foley stumbled back and fell on his butt. Just as his wife lunged at Finch, Courtney stuck her leg out and tripped the woman. Mrs. Foley crashed to the driveway in a disheveled heap.

The whole thing only took several seconds. The others stood on the porch gaping at the melee in the driveway.

"What do you have there?" Tom asked Finch.

Finch held a canvas in his hands and he unrolled a foot of it.

Angie gasped when she saw the colors and shapes. "It's…"

"The painting from my brother's living room." Finch glared at the Foleys.

"The stolen painting!" Ellie reached for the phone in her pocket, pulled it out, and called 911.

"Robbers." Anger contorted Mr. Finch's face. "Did you kill Thaddeus?"

The Foleys attempted to scramble away, but Tom blocked their escape and pushed them back onto the pavement of the driveway. He growled at them. "I'd stay where you are, if I were you."

Euclid sat on the porch railing looking smug.

Angie sidled up next to Ellie. "I bet the Foleys won't be leaving a five-star review for the B and B now."

* * *

After the police came to the Victorian and hauled the Foleys away, Tom, Finch, and the four sisters sat on the porch discussing what had just happened.

"Right under our noses." Ellie fumed. She got up and paced back and forth the length of the front porch. "That's great advertising for the B and B, isn't it? People will avoid coming here because they'll think we harbor criminals."

"You know," Courtney said, "people might be drawn to the excitement of staying at an inn where criminals visited."

Jenna rocked in her chair. "Maybe you should put that information on the B and B website. You can charge people extra to stay in the very room used by convicted felons."

Ellie groaned and plopped onto one of the chairs.

"How could murderers sit right at the table with us and none of us pick up on it?" Mr. Finch's face had lost its color. The exertion of wresting with the Foleys and the revelation of their misdeeds had worn him out.

Angie sat on the porch railing next to Euclid and Circe. "So the Foleys killed your brother and stole the artwork from his living room wall?" Something about it didn't seem right to her.

"It must have been an art deal gone wrong," Jenna speculated.

"I had several discussions about art with the Foleys." Finch sighed. "I never sensed that they were the killers."

Angie said, "Maybe because they're *not* the killers?"

Everyone turned towards Angie.

"What do you mean?" Tom asked. "The Foleys just stole the painting, but didn't murder Mr. Finch?" Tom glanced at Mr. Finch sitting near him. "The other Finch, not you."

Courtney rolled her eyes at Tom. "Obviously."

"It doesn't make sense to me." Angie slid from her sitting position on the railing and stood. "Suppose they killed candy store Finch. It seems pretty stupid to stay in Sweet Cove for so many days after the murder. Wouldn't you want to get away as soon as possible? Leave the area as soon as you could?"

"I think Angie's right." Courtney faced Mr. Finch. "Wouldn't we have picked up on their crime if they murdered your brother? Some small prick of suspicion? I bet we didn't sense that they stole the painting because we were so focused on figuring out who the killer is." She was careful how she worded her statements. Tom didn't know anything about the "gifts" that the Roseland sisters had started tapping into. Courtney didn't want to scare Tom away, so she danced around the issue.

Jenna said, "The cats didn't like the Foleys, but it wasn't an urgent sense of alarm like Euclid had that night last month when Professor Linden's murderer showed up here. Remember, Angie? Euclid practically chewed a hole through the kitchen door trying to get out. He knew Lisa Barrows was the killer. He never behaved that way when the Foleys were around. The cats had a more subtle dislike of them."

"The cats sense things?" Tom looked confused.

Angie said quickly, "The cats are a lot like dogs. You know, lots of dogs are good judges of character. They take a quick disliking to certain people. The cats do the same thing."

"I didn't know cats were like that." Tom gave the two felines admiring looks.

Angie's phone buzzed with an incoming text. She read the words and let out a sigh. "Chief Martin says it seems the Foleys have an iron clad alibi for the night of the murder."

"If the Foleys didn't kill Thaddeus," Mr. Finch asked, "then who did?"

21

The four sisters and Mr. Finch decided to have dinner together at the Pirate's Den on Main Street. Even though the restaurant was only a few blocks away, Ellie offered to drive everyone there in her van so that Mr. Finch wouldn't have to walk. Finch declined the offer. He said it was better to exercise his injured leg and if the girls wouldn't mind strolling at a leisurely pace, then he would enjoy walking to dinner.

The restaurant was crowded when they arrived, but Bessie, the owner, spotted the Roseland sisters and Mr. Finch as they entered, and she ushered the five of them to a table near the windows.

"This is most pleasant." Mr. Finch placed his napkin in his lap and perused the menu.

Lindsay, the assistant manager, came to the table to take their orders. She was wearing the earrings that she'd purchased from Jenna.

"They look great on you," Angie told Lindsay.

"I love them." Lindsay had her hair in a loose bun and the dangly earrings caught the light and sparkled. "I've had a million compliments on them." She nodded to Jenna. "I tell everyone where I bought them."

Jenna smiled. "I just made a necklace that would match those earrings. Come by the shop some day and I'll show you."

Lindsay frowned. "I'm here all the time now that business has picked up with the tourists. Could you come by with the jewelry some night after we close?"

Jenna offered to bring some new pieces of jewelry to the restaurant the next night and Lindsay readily agreed.

Ellie introduced Mr. Finch and tilted her head towards the candy shop across the street. "He and the other Mr. Finch were brothers."

Lindsay's smile faded as she eyed Finch.

Courtney whispered to her. "This Mr. Finch is nice."

Lindsay looked unsure. She pulled her order pad from the pocket of her apron. "Would you like to order appetizers?"

A woman's raspy voice called out. "Oh, look. It's the Roseland sisters."

They all turned to see Agnes and Mildred Walsh bustling towards their table. Lindsay let out a groan.

"Look at you all out together. It's hopping in here isn't it?" Mildred turned to Angie and Courtney. "Did you have any luck with that phone number we gave you from the dry cleaners?"

"It was a promising lead, but it turns out the man is innocent," Angie said.

"Ah. Too bad." Mildred glanced about the front dining room and waved and nodded to several people she knew.

Agnes smiled at Finch. "And who is this fine gentleman you have with you?"

Ellie introduced Mr. Finch as a B and B guest and left out his name in order to avoid the inevitable comparison between this Finch and the dead one.

Mildred was about to press for their guest's name when Bessie arrived with menus and showed the Walsh sisters to a table on the other side of the room.

"Those two." Lindsay scowled. "They're always up in everyone's business. Such busybodies." She leaned down. "And they are such complainers. I'm glad they're not sitting at one of my tables tonight. When they worked at the candy store, they were in here all the time. I dreaded waiting on them."

"They have forceful personalities, for sure." Angie grinned.

The girls and Finch ordered their meals and shared nachos for an appetizer.

"There's quite a good view of my brother's candy store from here." Mr. Finch looked out the restaurant window.

Angie followed Finch's gaze. The now familiar thrumming started beating in her veins. After only a few pulses, the sensation faded away.

Courtney shot Angie a look. "What is it?"

Angie met her sister's eyes. "What do you mean?"

"I felt something from you."

"The thrumming started." Angie kept her voice low.

Courtney's eyes narrowed. "Do you still feel it?"

Angie shook her head.

"I felt it, too, but it was coming from you," Courtney said.

Finch looked from sister to sister. "What's going on?"

Jenna explained as best she could. Finch looked impressed.

Ellie blinked. She was sitting ramrod straight. She asked warily, "What did you feel?"

Angie took a gulp from her water glass. "I looked across the street at the candy store. The thrumming started up, but it faded really fast." She took a quick look around the busy dining room. Her heart was beating double-time. "It has something to do with this restaurant."

"What could it be?" Ellie twisted a strand of her long blonde hair. She seemed like she might get up and flee.

"Is the killer in here?" Courtney whispered. "We should go get the cats."

"I don't think they'd allow cats in here," Finch observed.

Jenna made a suggestion to Angie. "Look out the window again. Look at the candy store. Does the thrumming start again?"

Angie trained her eyes on the building across the street. She waited for something to start in her blood. She shook her head. "Nothing."

Jenna let out a sigh. "Why are these abilities such a puzzle? Why are they shrouded in mystery? Why can't the stupid powers be more straightforward?"

Courtney glanced over her shoulder. "It has to be someone in here. Either the killer is in here or someone here knows who the killer is."

"How can we figure it out?" Jenna whispered. "I wish

we could lock the restaurant door and keep everyone from leaving."

They were so engrossed in the conversation that they didn't hear Lindsay come over to the table. "Want anything else?"

Ellie jumped. "No," she said quickly. "Just the bill."

Lindsay removed their bill from her order pad.

Mr. Finch held out his hand. "I'll take that. It's my treat."

The girls protested but Finch insisted. Lindsay passed him the piece of paper with the charges written on it and then she moved to the next table. Mr. Finch opened his billfold, removed some cash, and counted out the necessary amount which he placed in the middle of the table. The five of them got up and left the restaurant. They started down the sidewalk back to the Victorian. Stars sparkled in the sky. The main street was crowded with people heading out to browse the stores or to eat in the many restaurants that lined the center of Sweet Cove.

"How will we ever figure out who the killer is?" Courtney moaned.

Mr. Finch leaned on his cane. "Talk to our waitress."

Under a streetlamp, the four sisters stopped short and stared at Finch.

"She handed me the bill," Finch said. "We held it at the same time. Something passed to me." He held each of the girls' eyes. "She knows."

22

Chief Martin sat in the living room of the Victorian with Angie, Jenna, Courtney, and Finch. Ellie had just finished cleaning up the kitchen from the morning breakfast preparations. She hurried to join the group. Euclid and Circe lay curled up on the rug in front of the fireplace.

"The Foley's have been charged with stealing the painting from your brother's home. We'd like to hold onto it for a few more days if you don't mind, Mr. Finch."

Finch sat straight in a side chair. He held the top of his cane with both hands. "I have no intention of keeping that painting. I plan to donate it to the Museum of Fine Arts in Boston, unless you discover that it is stolen property. Which wouldn't surprise me in the least."

"That's very generous of you, Mr. Finch." The chief rubbed his forehead. "As I mentioned, the Foleys have an alibi for the night your brother was murdered. They were at the resort having dinner late that night and then they spent several hours at the bar. A number of people are able to vouch for them."

Finch nodded slightly. "I see."

The chief went on. "They did visit the candy store prior to going to dinner. They mentioned seeing the resort manager in the store at the same time, and they also noted that Finch sent his regular employee home early. This was because the Foley's had arranged with Finch to make a purchase from him, other than candy. Finch had brokered an art deal for the Foleys that didn't come to fruition. The Foleys had sent Finch a deposit. Finch refused to return the money to the Foleys, saying it was his fee for his troubles. It was quite a large sum. They argued. Finch threatened to badmouth them to his art world contacts. He planned to make sure that the Foleys would be blacklisted from any future private art deals." The chief cleared his throat. "When the Foleys heard that Finch had been murdered, they hatched the plan to go to his house and steal some artwork from him. They claim they were justified since your brother owed them money."

Finch clutched tightly to his cane. "So many unscrupulous people in the world."

Chief Martin nodded. "I want to assure you that we continue to work to find your brother's killer."

"Thank you, Chief Martin," Finch said. "I hope that your investigation will prove fruitful soon. In my opinion, my brother was a blight on humanity. But it is also my belief that no one deserves to be murdered. I hope you find the killer, not for Thaddeus' sake, but to keep the good people of Sweet Cove safe."

Chief Martin said, "We'll do all we can."

The chief made a move to get up to leave when Angie cleared her throat. "Um. Chief, we want to tell you something."

Chief Martin turned expectant eyes to Angie.

Angie, Jenna, Courtney, and Finch took turns relaying what had happened the previous night at the restaurant. Ellie stayed quiet. Euclid and Circe both sat up, listening with interest.

"I have a strong feeling that our waitress has knowledge about the crime," Finch said.

"Hmm." Chief Martin looked across the room, thinking. "It might be a good idea to talk to Lindsay again."

"You know." Jenna leaned forward in her seat. "I've walked by the Pirate's Den late at night. I've seen Lindsay sitting near the window after the restaurant is closed. She goes over the evening receipts and cashes out the register to reconcile the money from the night's business."

Ellie's eyes widened and she almost jumped up from her chair. "I've seen Lindsay in there at night, too. Every time I've seen her, she's sitting at the table that we all sat at last night. She always sits by the window." Ellie looked straight at Angie. "In the seat you were sitting in last night."

Courtney turned to Angie. "That's why you felt something during dinner. I bet Lindsay saw something or someone the night Finch was killed. She had a direct view of the front of the candy shop. You picked up on it. That's what the thrumming was trying to tell you."

Euclid arched his back and let out a low hiss.

Chief Martin stood up. "I think I'll pay Lindsay a visit right away." He thanked the girls and shook hands with Finch. Courtney showed him to the door.

Before Courtney could return to her seat, the doorbell chimed. "I'll get it. The chief probably forgot something." When she opened the door, Betty Hayes stood on the porch.

"Hello, Courtney." Betty brushed past and entered the foyer. "Is Victor here?"

Courtney looked blank for a moment, and then said, "Oh, you mean Mr. Finch."

Finch heard Betty's voice and came into the foyer to greet her.

Betty beamed at him. "Oh, there you are. You're looking very nice today, Victor."

"And so are you, Miss Betty." Despite Finch's limp, he had a spring in his step whenever Betty was around. Courtney had to stifle a chuckle at the way the two of them oogled one another.

"A small ranch has just come on the market." Betty batted her eyelashes at Finch. "It's adorable. I think it's perfect for you. Do you have time to see it? It's just around the corner from here on a lovely side street. We should jump on this. It will go quickly."

"I'd love to see it." Finch's cheeks were flushed with a healthy glow.

Betty said to Courtney, "Victor tells me he's been teaching you to make candy. He says you're a natural."

"She is indeed." Mr. Finch smiled.

Betty eyed Courtney. "You know, you should think about running a candy business. You could take over Finch's shop. We can't have Sweet Cove without a candy store. The lease is coming available very soon."

Courtney said, "I thought Lindsay Cooper wanted to open a sandwich shop in the space."

Betty swatted the air with her hand. "Oh, her. Maybe." Betty plastered on her sweet smile. "The candy store is in a wonderful location. A spot like that doesn't come along very often." She patted Courtney's arm. "Think about it. You're done with college now. Your sisters are all entrepreneurs. You may as well be one too."

"Perhaps I could treat you to lunch after we take a look at the ranch?" Finch held Betty's elbow and the two opened the front door and headed to her car.

Euclid and Circe jumped onto the side table near the window so that they could watch Finch and Betty leave.

When the door closed, Courtney turned to her sisters. "Those two. Who would have guessed?"

Jenna accused Angie. "Did you put a love spell in something those two ate?"

They laughed.

"Do you think Lindsay changed her mind about the sandwich shop?" Jenna asked. "She sure seemed gung ho when she told us about it."

Courtney sat down on the sofa next to Angie. "Maybe she decided she didn't want her shop in a place where a guy was murdered."

"Or maybe Betty is trying to start a bidding war for the lease," Angie suggested. "I wouldn't put it past her."

Ellie asked Courtney, "What do you think about what Betty suggested?"

"The candy shop? I don't know anything about running a business." Courtney patted Circe who had curled next to her.

"You could learn." Ellie got up to return to the kitchen. "Think about it."

Jenna stood up too. "Enough sitting around. Some of us have to work." She headed to her jewelry shop at the back of the house.

"Come on," Angie squeezed Courtney's shoulder. "We promised Ellie we'd clean the guest rooms and bathrooms today."

As they climbed the stairs, Courtney groaned. "Not my favorite activity. I'd better seriously consider becoming a candy maker."

* * *

During dinner, Jenna told her sisters she was going to the Pirate's Den later in the evening to show Lindsay some new jewelry and asked if anyone wanted go with her. Jenna planned to sit with Lindsay at the restaurant and show her some pieces once the customers were gone and it was closed for the night.

"I'll go." Courtney helped clear the dinner dishes from the dining table.

"I'm meeting Attorney Ford in an hour to finish going over the business papers he's drawn up for the B and B." Ellie finished her tea. "After that, I'm taking a shower and going to bed. I'm beat."

Courtney raised an eyebrow. "An evening meeting?"

Ellie yawned. "We're both busy people."

"You want to come, Angie?" Jenna asked. "We could go and have a drink and an appetizer while we wait for Lindsay to finish up. Maybe we can get her to tell what she knows about dead Finch's murder."

"I guess so." Angie rubbed her forehead. "I've had a headache ever since I had that thrumming at dinner last night. I hope it doesn't happen again when we're there." She didn't know why, but a wave of unease washed over her.

23

Jenna, Angie, and Courtney headed into the center of Sweet Cove. Jenna carried a small briefcase with her new jewelry designs inside. The night was clear and the air retained the warmth of the day. A full moon glowed in the ebony sky.

"How's your headache?" Jenna asked her sister.

"I still have it." Angie had taken a nap after dinner hoping that sleeping for a little while would ease the throbbing in her head.

"Maybe a good night's sleep will help."

The girls entered the Pirate's Den. Most of the tables were filled with customers. Bessie, the owner, spotted them and hurried over. "Lindsay went home. She was afraid she was getting a migraine and her medicine was in her apartment. She told me to tell you to come over. Here's her address. She lives just a half mile from here." Bessie handed Jenna a piece of paper with the address on it.

The girls thanked Bessie and stepped outside.

"You okay with walking to Lindsay's place?" Jenna asked her sisters.

"Fine with me," Angie said. "The restaurant was really crowded. I don't mind avoiding all the noise in there."

"Let's go, then." Courtney turned to lead the way.

Angie glanced at the darkened candy shop across the street as they walked along the sidewalk away from the restaurant. A shiver traveled down her spine.

After a ten-minute walk on the side streets of Sweet Cove, the sisters stopped in front of an historic home. "This is it." Jenna led the way up to the front door of the three story stone house. There were three doorbells on the side of the door with names printed on pieces of paper that were slipped into brass holders. "Here's Lindsay's." Jenna pressed the button. After a few minutes, the front door opened. Lindsay greeted them wearing a pullover sweater and loose black slacks.

"Hope you didn't mind coming here." Lindsay led the girls to her second floor apartment. "I had to take my migraine medicine before the headache kicked in."

Angie had a vague sense of unease as she climbed the stairs. Waiting for Lindsay to open the apartment door, she took a quick look at Courtney to see if she might be displaying any signs of discomfort or reservation.

Lindsay swung the door open. The living area was decorated with a large cream colored sofa, two club chairs in a light shade of chocolate, and a glass coffee table placed on a rug with a contemporary design. A large white wall unit was placed on one side of the room and several of the shelves were filled with hardcover books. Green plants stood here and there about the room. Framed photographs of nature scenes hung on the walls.

"What a nice place," Courtney said admiring the space.

"You can spread the jewelry on the table." Lindsay gestured to the coffee table. "How about some cold drinks?"

Jenna opened her case of jewelry and began placing the pieces on suede mats that she'd brought along to use to display the designs. Angie took a seat on the sofa while Courtney walked around the room looking at the photographs on the walls.

Lindsay headed to the kitchen to get the drinks. "I used to enjoy dabbling in photography. I don't have the time anymore, but I'd like to get back to it someday."

A bead of cold sweat ran down Angie's back. Her heart pounded. She wondered if she might be coming down with the flu.

"I can't wait to see the new pieces," Lindsay called from the kitchen. The girls could hear her placing ice cubes in glasses.

Courtney stood in front of the bookcase reading the titles on the spines of the books. Most of the them fell into the category of the classics. "You have a great collection of books." She reached for a leather bound volume. "This one looks really old."

A crash sounded from the kitchen as a glass hit the tile floor and shattered. Lindsay rushed into the living area. Her voice was high. "Will you come here and help me, Courtney?"

Jenna turned towards Lindsay.

Angie's head pounded like it was about to explode and with each beat of her heart, her blood thrummed. *What's wrong here?*

Courtney slowly lifted her eyes from the thick, heavy book she held in her hands. She glared at Lindsay. "You."

Angie's body flooded with panic. She leaped up and rushed across the room to her sister's side, sensing that Courtney was in danger.

Jenna's body stiffened from the tension in the room. "What? What's going on?" Her gaze darted from Lindsay to her sisters.

Courtney's tone dripped with disgust. "This is Mr. Finch's recipe book."

Lindsay's face hardened. She took several steps to a desk near the side wall, never taking her eyes off the girls. She pulled open the desk drawer and removed a gun.

Angie clutched Courtney's arm, pulled her back, and instinctively moved in front of her. Jenna edged closer to her sisters.

"You killed him." Angie narrowed her eyes.

"Yes, I killed him. That monster." Lindsay's face muscles tightened. "He deserved to die. He made my life hell. He lied that I stole from him. Everyone hated him. I figured out he was dealing in art." Lindsay raised the barrel of the gun. "I confronted him. I told him I'd go to the police with the information. I wanted money to keep quiet." She let out a shrill cackle. "That greedy monster. He refused. So I stabbed him with his own kitchen knife. I robbed his safe. In the end, he was right. I did steal from him."

"Lindsay...." Angie took a step forward.

"Don't move," Lindsay ordered.

Angie held her hands out, the palms facing Lindsay. "We'll leave. We'll wait before going to the police so you have plenty of time to get away." Her voice shook even though she tried to keep it steady.

Lindsay snorted. "I don't think so."

Suddenly a strange sensation of relief washed over Angie. She listened.

Lindsay waved the gun. "Come on, the three of you. Get in my bedroom."

The girls stood still.

Lindsay shrieked. "Move!"

Angie's muscles tensed. *Get ready. They're coming.*

The apartment door cracked and splintered from a heavy boot's impact and it flew open, just as Angie turned and knocked Courtney to the floor. "Get down, Jenna!" Angie yelled as she and Courtney fell.

Two gunshots rang through the apartment.

Out of the corner of her eye, Angie saw Chief Martin and a second police officer in the room, their guns drawn and pointed towards the spot where Lindsay had been standing. Two other officers ran in from the back door. Lindsay's curses burned into Angie's ears. The murderer wailed and screamed as the police cuffed her and hauled her away.

Chief Martin ran to the girls. The three of them hauled themselves up off the floor. Relief spread over the chief's face. "You scared me there for a second."

Angie's stomach clenched and her head was spinning. She crumpled onto the sofa and put her head on her knees, her hair falling over her face.

"Take deep breaths." Courtney rubbed Angie's shoulders.

Jenna sat down beside Angie and put her hand on her twin sister's arm. Tears gathered in her eyes. She rested her cheek against Angie's back.

With her head still on her knees, Angie asked the chief, "How did you know we were here?"

Chief Martin gently slid the jewelry to the side and sat down on the glass coffee table in front of the girls. "Ellie. She called us. She'd called the Pirate's Den, they told her you were here. When Ellie got home from meeting Attorney Ford, the cats were going berserk in the house. Screaming, jumping over the furniture, climbing up the drapes. Ellie knew you were in danger."

Angie said softly, "Once again, saved by felines."

"And by Ellie's quick thinking," Jenna added.

The coffee table creaked under the chief's weight and the glass panel beneath his butt shifted and slipped from the metal sides. The panel and the chief collapsed onto the rug with an impressive thud. Angie lifted her head to see Chief Martin sprawled on the floor.

Laughter spilled from the girls' throats. Jenna and Courtney each gripped one of the chief's arms and hauled the red-faced man to his feet.

24

The police took Lindsay into custody and charged her with the murder of Mr. Thaddeus Finch. Working at the Pirate's Den and sitting near the window each night reconciling the evening's receipts, Lindsay had a good view of the goings-on in Finch's candy store. She noticed parcels being delivered to the shop early some mornings and late some nights. Her regular jogging route ended right in front of Finch's store and one day, she heard Finch arguing with people about a piece of art.

Lindsay watched the activities at the candy store with a close eye and figured out that Finch must be dealing in artwork. Her discovery of his secret, in combination with her hatred for the man, ignited the plan to blackmail Finch. When the confrontation with Finch went sour, Lindsay ended up stabbing him to death. She stole hundreds of thousands of dollars from the store safe and from Finch's home.

After Chief Martin and his officers rescued the sisters from Lindsay's apartment, the Chief directed his men to haul the murderer off to the Sweet Cove jail. Chief Martin then drove the girls back to their home, the headlights of his car cutting through the darkness like little beacons.

Ellie, Mr. Finch, and the two cats stood under the Victorian's front porch light, their faces tight and worried, as the police cruiser pulled into the driveway. Tears streamed from Ellie's eyes when she saw Courtney, Jenna, and Angie emerge unhurt from the vehicle. Mr. Finch clapped his hands with joy and Euclid and Circe rushed down the steps and danced around the sisters. Chief Martin had tied a jacket around his waist to hide the huge rip in his trousers that was caused by his undignified fall through the glass coffee table.

Courtney carried the old, leather bound book that she'd discovered in Lindsay's apartment. She clutched it tight to her chest and climbed up to the porch where she handed it to Mr. Finch. "It's your grandmother's recipe book. Lindsay stole it from your brother's store. Now it's back where it belongs."

Mr. Finch reached for the book with shaking hands. He reverently passed his palm over the leather cover. Tears spilled from his eyes and his body shook. Courtney wrapped him in her arms.

* * *

Two weeks had passed since Lindsay Cooper pointed a gun at Angie, Jenna, and Courtney and threatened to kill them. Slowly, things had returned to normal.

Angie and her sisters walked up Beach Street and into

the Victorian for lunch. They had finally been able to spend a few hours on Sweet Cove beach where they used boogie boards in the waves and sunned themselves on the sand.

The girls sat around the dining room table eating sandwiches and salad. Euclid and Circe each enjoyed some tuna fish on their own small plates placed on the floor at the side of the room. Ever since the cats had alerted Ellie that her three sisters were in danger, everyone in the household treated Euclid and Circe like royalty, although that was how they were usually treated anyway.

Mr. Finch opened the front door and smiled broadly at the group gathered around the table. "Hello. I was afraid I was late."

Angie swallowed a bite of her sandwich. "Late for what?"

Ellie caught Finch's eye and shook her head being careful that Angie didn't notice.

"Um." Finch removed his jacket. "Lunch. I thought I might miss lunch." He joined the girls at the table. "Everything is all set for me to close on the ranch house next week." Finch had made an offer to buy a small ranch-style house located on a quiet, side street of Sweet Cove just a few blocks from the Victorian.

"We're very glad that you're going to be a permanent resident of Sweet Cove." Ellie passed Finch a platter of cheeses, meats, sliced tomatoes, pickles, and lettuce so that he could make a sandwich.

"We'll have to celebrate with a get-together once I close on the house." Finch took a freshly baked roll from the basket and cut it in half. "I'll have all of you over for a nice dinner once I move in. The cats, too."

The doorbell rang and Jenna, Ellie, Courtney, and Finch

glanced at each other and tried to suppress smiles.

"Who could that be?" Angie rose from her seat and walked into the foyer. She opened the door to see Attorney Ford.

"Hello, Ms. Roseland. May I come in?" Ford wore a light gray linen jacket. His bow tie was flaming red.

Angie stepped back to let Ford enter the room. She wondered why he had come to the house. "Do you have an appointment to see Ellie for something?"

Ford's face was serious. "Ah, no. I need to speak with you about the legal proceedings for the Victorian."

Angie's heart dropped. "Is something wrong? Is there a problem with the will?"

"Could we sit down and talk?" Ford looked into the living room.

Angie led Ford to the sofas. Her stomach felt like it was full of ice water. *What's gone wrong?*

Angie's sisters and Finch disappeared into the kitchen.

Ford opened his briefcase and slipped a folder out. He held Angie's eyes. His face was somber. "It's about the transfer of the Victorian to you." He cleared his throat.

"What's wrong?" Angie sat with her hands clutched together in her lap. Her heart pounded.

Ford removed an envelope from the folder. He glanced into the foyer before handing it to Angie. "Congratulations, Ms. Roseland. You are the official owner of this fine home."

Angie blinked.

"Congratulations!" Happy shouts from her sisters and Mr. Finch filled the room as they rushed into the living room. Ellie carried a cake. Mr. Finch had a bouquet of multi-colored balloons clutched in his hand. Courtney carried a tray with glasses and plates and Jenna held a bottle of champagne. Euclid and Circe jumped on the sofa beside Angie. Courtney and Jenna ran to their sister and bear-hugged her.

Tears gathered in Angie's eyes. "You all knew?" she blubbered.

"Attorney Ford told me yesterday." Ellie placed the cake on the coffee table and she hugged Angie. "He thought we might want to know ahead of time so we could surprise you with some champagne."

Angie stared at the envelope in her hands. She lifted her eyes to Ford. "Really? It's done?"

Ford nodded. "The copy of the deed is enclosed in the envelope. The bank check for seventy-five thousand dollars is also in the envelope."

Tears streamed down Angie's face. "I can't believe it."

The front door opened and Tom walked in carrying his tool case. "You'd better believe it." He smiled. "I'm starting the renovations for your bake shop today." He placed the tool case on the foyer floor. "But first, I need a glass of champagne."

A loud pop announced the opening of the bottle and Ellie poured the sparkling liquid into all of the glasses. She handed one to Angie. "I think you should make a toast."

Angie brushed tears from her cheeks. "Well." She coughed to try to clear the emotion from her voice and she held tight to the envelope containing the deed. She pressed it to her chest. "First of all ... to Professor Marion Linden, for giving us all the gift of this beautiful, Victorian home." She looked around at everyone. "To all of you ... and to happy days ahead for all of us." Angie looked over at the cats. She smiled and raised her glass to them. "And, to our two fabulous felines."

Everyone cheered and took sips from their glasses. Ellie cut the cake and passed the slices around. The doorbell rang. Courtney answered it and returned to the living room carrying a gigantic bouquet of flowers. "Guess who these are for?" She placed them on the coffee table in front of Angie.

"Who sent them?" Angie reached for the card. She read it and her cheeks flushed. "They're from Josh."

"What does he say?" Jenna asked. Angie passed the card to her and Jenna read it aloud. *"Congratulations, Angie! Sorry I can't be there with you today, but how about a celebratory dinner when I get back to Sweet Cove? Love, Josh."*

"Love? Love, Josh?" Courtney teased. "Well, well."

A brighter pink flushed Angie's cheeks. "Oh, hush you."

They ate cake and sipped the champagne and chatted with each other.

"I'm planning on being done with the renovations in four weeks." Tom accepted another piece of cake from Ellie. "You'll be able to open your bake shop before August," he told Angie.

"I can't believe it." Angie collapsed on the sofa. "I'm overwhelmed."

Jenna leaned against the sofa back and took a bite of her cake. "I'm looking forward to everything settling down and all of us having a nice, quiet summer."

Courtney chuckled. "Things settling down? Is that even possible in this family?" She sat on the floor next to the cats and allowed each one a tiny lick of frosting.

Tom stood up. "If Angie is going to open her shop soon, then I'd better get to work. Enough goofing off." He carried his empty plate to the kitchen.

Attorney Ford chatted with Ellie near the fireplace and when he finished his cake, he said, "I'd better get back to the office." Ford retrieved his briefcase and said goodbye to everyone. Angie stood up and walked the attorney out to the front porch.

"Best wishes for your new home, Ms. Roseland."

"Thank you for your help," Angie said.

Attorney Ford started down the steps, but stopped abruptly. "I almost forgot." He reached into his briefcase and removed a small book. "I spoke with my uncle the other day. He's enjoying his retirement in Florida. He told me about this." Ford handed the book to Angie. "The historical society put it together for Sweet Cove's three-hundred-and-seventy-fifth anniversary celebration. I thought you might find it interesting."

Angie held the publication and looked at the cover.

"It has some historical information about Robin's Point." Ford held Angie's eyes. "There's also a little bit in there about Professor Linden's father."

Angie blinked. She couldn't help feeling surprised that Ford brought the book for her to read. "Thank you," she told him softly.

"My uncle and I had a long chat. Things are clearer to me."

Angie tilted her head. She wasn't sure what the attorney meant, but she could feel warmth coming from him now.

Ford adjusted his glasses. "Have you had time to find

out anything about Professor Linden's father? I know you have an interest in him."

"No. With everything going on, we haven't had a chance to do any research."

"Well, maybe this book will be a beginning." Ford turned to go down the steps. "Have a nice day, Ms. Roseland."

"Attorney Ford...." Angie said.

Ford turned back to her.

"Call me Angie."

The corners of the attorney's mouth turned up. He held out his hand to her. "Call me Jack."

They shook hands and Angie smiled at him. Watching Ford walk away from the Victorian, Angie still had loads of questions, but she had the feeling that one day they'd all be answered.

Circe jumped up on the porch rail and Angie turned to the cat. "You know what? Sometimes people can surprise you." She reached her hand to scratch Circe's cheek. The cat turned her face so both cheeks would receive equal attention. Purring filled the air.

The smash of Tom's sledgehammer hitting the den wall inside the house made Angie jump. She chuckled. "You're about to get your wish, Circe. Tom's breaking through the den wall into the kitchen. Let's go see if there's any evidence of mice hiding in there. Then that mystery will be solved."

The black cat trilled. She leaped down from the rail, landed softly on the porch, and led the way through the open front door into the Victorian.

Angie's Victorian.

ABOUT THE AUTHOR

Thank you for reading!

J.A. Whiting lives with her family in New England where she works full time in education. Whiting loves reading and writing mystery and suspense stories.

Visit her at:

http://www.jawhitingbooks.com/
www.facebook.com/jawhitingauthor
www.amazon.com/author/jawhiting

Check out more of J.A. Whiting's books at:

www.amazon.com/author/jawhiting

To hear about new books and book sales, please sign up for her mailing list at:

http://www.jawhitingbooks.com

Your email will never be sold, shared, or spammed.

SOME RECIPES FROM

THE SWEET DREAMS
BED AND BREAKFAST INN

BLUEBERRY MUFFINS

Ingredients:

Streusel:

- ½ cup (100 g) of packed (dark or light brown) sugar
- ½ cup (67g) pecans or walnuts, chopped – use either kind of nut or a mix the two kinds of nuts, or leave them out entirely if you aren't a nut person
- 1 teaspoon of ground cinnamon

Muffins:

- ½ cup (115g) of unsalted butter, softened
- ½ cup (100g) of granulated sugar
- ¼ cup (50g) of either dark or light brown sugar
- 2 large eggs, room temperature is best
- ½ cup (120g) yogurt (Greek or whatever kind you like; you can also use
- vanilla or blueberry yogurt; if you prefer, you can replace the yogurt
- with sour cream)
- 2 teaspoons of vanilla extract

- 1 ¾ cups (220g) of all-purpose flour
- 1 teaspoon baking soda
- 1 teaspoon baking powder
- ½ teaspoon salt
- ¼ cup (60ml) milk (whichever kind you prefer)
- 1 ½ cups (250g) of fresh or frozen blueberries (do not thaw) – or use a mixture or fresh and frozen blueberries

Note: You can use any favorite fruit in place of the blueberries

Directions:

- Preheat the oven to 425 degrees
- Spray two 12-count muffin tins with non-stick spray or line the muffin tins with muffin/cupcake liners (there will be enough batter to make 14 muffins)

Prepare the Steusel:

- In a bowl, mix together brown sugar, nuts and cinnamon

Prepare the Muffins:

- In a medium sized bowl, beat the butter on high until smooth and creamy (takes about 1 minute)
- Add the granulated sugar and brown sugar and beat on high until creamed (takes about 2 minutes)

- Add the eggs, vanilla, and yogurt (or sour cream)
- Beat on medium speed for about 1 minute, and then increase the speed to high until the mixture is well-combined and has a nice uniform texture
- In a large bowl, blend together the flour, baking soda, baking powder, and salt until well mixed
- Pour the wet ingredients into the large bowl containing the dry ingredients. Mix with a whisk
- Add the milk, whisk slowly until combined and there are still some lumps Gently fold in the blueberries with a rubber spatula or a wooden spoon; It's okay if some blueberry juice escapes into the batter
- Layer the batter and the streusel – Place 1 tablespoon of batter into the muffin tin, sprinkle in a little streusel, then another layer of the batter, etc, ending with some streusel on top. Bring the layers all the way to the top of the tins (this will make a nice tall muffin)
- Bake the muffins for 5 minutes at 425 degrees then lower the temperature to 350 degrees (leave the muffins in the oven when you change the temp) and bake for about 23-26 more minutes

Note: Reducing the temperature should cause the tops of the muffins to pop up into a nice dome-shape.

Cool

Note: Muffins can stay at room temp up to 5 days; you can freeze them for up to 2 months !

HAZELNUT CAKE

Ingredients:

- 25 ounces (or 250 g) of ground hazelnuts (can also be mixed with some ground walnuts)
- ¾ cup of sugar
- 4 drops of almond extract
- 2 cups of flour
- 4 teaspoons baking powder
- 1 cup plus 2 ounces of milk

Directions:

- Mix hazelnuts with the sugar
- Mix flour with the baking powder
- Add the two mixtures together and blend well
- Add almond extract and milk, and blend together with dry ingredients
- Butter a loaf pan
- Transfer the mixture to the loaf pan
- Bake 45 minutes at 325 degrees – Then turn up to 350 degrees for 5 more minutes
- Cool and frost with your favorite frosting or sprinkle with confectioner's sugar

CHOCOLATE BROWNIE COOKIES (RICH!)

Ingredients:

- 1 cup flour
- 1 teaspoon baking soda
- ½ teaspoon salt
- ½ cup (1 stick) unsalted butter – cut up into chunks

- 8 ounces of semisweet chocolate, chopped up coarsely
- 4 ounces of unsweetened chocolate, chopped up coarsely
- 4 eggs
- 1 cup light brown sugar
- ½ cup granulated sugar
- 1 teaspoon vanilla extract
- 1 cup semisweet chocolate chips
- Confectioner's sugar to sprinkle on the cookies

Directions:

- In a bowl, mix flour, baking powder, and salt to blend
- In a saucepan, combine butter and the semisweet and unsweetened chocolate. Melt together over low heat. Set aside
- In another large bowl, beat the eggs with the brown sugar and granulated sugar for 1 minute; beat in the vanilla, then the chocolate mixture
- Stir in the flour mixture – combine well
- Stir in the semisweet chocolate chips
- Scrape down the sides of the bowl and cover with plastic wrap *Refrigerate the mixture for at least 30 minutes (can refrigerate for up to 2 hours)
- Set oven to 350 degrees
- Line cookie sheets with parchment paper
- Using a 2-tablespoon capacity ice cream scoop or two large spoons, scoop mounds of the batter onto the baking sheet, leave 2 inches between each mound
- Bake the cookies for 14 minutes or until the tops are just firm when pressed lightly with a fingertip (they will firm up when they cool)

- Cool the cookies on wire racks
- When completely cool, sprinkle the tops with confectioner's sugar

Adapted from a 2011 Boston Globe recipe

HOMEMADE GRANOLA BARS

Ingredients:

- 1 ½ cups slivered almonds
- 1 ½ cups dried tart cherries
- 1 ½ cups of old-fashioned rolled oats
- ½ cup flour
- ½ cup wheat germ
- ¼ teaspoon salt
- ¼ cup canola oil
- 2/3 cup honey
- 1 teaspoon vanilla extract
- 2/3 cup dark chocolate chips

Directions:

- Set oven to 350 degrees
- Line a 9 inch square pan with parchment paper (be sure there is enough paper to come up above the sides by at least an inch)
- On a baking sheet, spread out the almonds in a single layer
- Bake the almonds for 7 minutes or until golden brown, turn once or twice. Set aside and let cool completely
- In a food processor, pulse the cherries and almonds until the almonds are chopped but not powdery

- In a large bowl, combine the cherry mixture with the oats, flour, wheat germ and salt
- Add the oil, honey, vanilla, and chips. Stir with rubber spatula to blend well
- Transfer the batter to the pan using the spatula to press it evenly in the pan
- Bake for 40 minutes or until the center is firm when pressed with a fingertip and the edges begin to brown
- Transfer the pan to wire rack to cool
- Use the ends of the parchment paper like handles and lift the bars from the pan; transfer to a cutting board
- Cut the square in half, then cut each rectangle into 6 pieces to form 12 bars

Adapted from 2013 Boston Globe recipe

ONE CRUST PECAN PIE (USE 8 INCH PIE PLATE)

Ingredients for the pie crust:

- 2 1/4 cups of flour
- 1 teaspoon of salt
- 3/4 cup plus 2 tablespoons of shortening – you may substitute the shortening with either: the same amount of butter or substitute with a little less than ¾ cup of canola oil
- 1/4 cup of boiling water
- 1 tablespoon of milk

Directions for the pie crust:

- In a medium bowl, sift together the flour and salt

- In a medium bowl, mix together shortening, boiling water, and milk
- Pour flour mixture into shortening mixture and stir with a fork, combining quickly until the mixture is the size of peas
- Roll out the crust between two pieces of wax paper (it helps to wet the counter in order to keep the paper from moving) – there will be more crust than you need
- Place the crust in the pie pan letting the crust overhang the edges of the pan
- Ingredients for the filling:
- ¼ cup butter (or replace with 3 tablespoons canola oil)
- 2/3 cup of firmly packed brown sugar
- ¾ cup dark corn syrup
- 3 eggs well beaten
- Dash of salt
- 1 cup of pecan halves
- 1 teaspoon vanilla

Directions for the filling:

- Cream the butter (or oil), sugar, and salt
- Stir in the remaining ingredients
- Place in the pastry crust
- Trim the edges of the crust to remove the excess
- Bake at 450 degrees for 10 minutes, then turn the temperature to 350 degrees and bake for 30-35 minutes or until a knife inserted comes out clean

GINGER - MOLASSES COOKIES

Ingredients:

- 2 ¼ cups of all-purpose flour

- 2 teaspoons of ground ginger
- 1 teaspoon baking soda
- ¾ teaspoon of ground cinnamon
- ½ teaspoon of ground cloves
- ¼ teaspoon of salt
- ¾ cup butter, softened
- 1 cup of granulated sugar
- 1 egg
- 1 tablespoon water
- ¼ cup molasses
- 2 tablespoons granulated sugar to roll the cookie balls in

Directions:

- Set oven to 350 degrees
- Blend together flour, ginger, baking soda, cinnamon, cloves, and salt
- In a large bowl, beat together the butter and 1 cup granulated sugar until light and fluffy
- Beat in the egg
- Stir in the water and molasses
- Gradually stir the mixed dry ingredients into the molasses mixture
- Shape the dough into small balls and roll them in the 2 tablespoons of the sugar
- Place cookies on an ungreased cookie sheet about 2 inches apart; Slightly flatten each cookie
- Bake in the preheated oven for 8-10 minutes
- Cool on the baking sheet for 5 minutes before moving the cookies to a wire rack to finish cooling

Made in the USA
Middletown, DE
06 February 2024

49197890R00120